a forbidden royal romance

DIRTY
HALO

evie east

Cover design by: ONE CLICK COVERS
www.oneclickcovers.com

Subscribe to Evie's monthly BOOK BLAST:
http://eepurl.com/dyjGAr

For T.S.

"My castle crumbled overnight
I brought a knife to a gunfight
They took the crown, but it's alright..."

"CALL IT WHAT YOU WANT" BY TAYLOR SWIFT

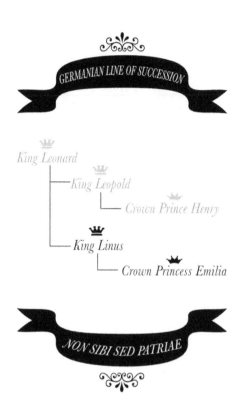

GERMANIAN LINE OF SUCCESSION

King Leonard
  ├── King Leopold
  │   └── Crown Prince Henry
  └── King Linus
        └── Crown Princess Emilia

NON SIBI SED PATRIAE

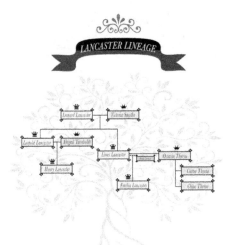

LANCASTER

non sibi sed patriae

My dear reader,

DIRTY HALO is a dark fairy tale intended only for adults. If you prefer your fairy tales without prolific swearing, intense royal scheming, and scorching hot sex, I suggest you turn back now. Stick to the animated cartoon versions on your TV screen.

As for the rest of you depraved souls...

I hope you enjoy Emilia's journey from ordinary girl to unwilling princess. Many aspects of this tale, from settings to character profiles, are based loosely on both historical account and folklore. However, I feel it is my duty to inform you that the kingdom of Germania — a small yet prosperous country wedged on the border between Germany, Austria, and Switzerland — is not, in fact, a real place. (You know, just so you don't book a plane ticket there to track down a certain smirking, smoldering Lord.)

And now, without further ado...
  WAIT!
  I'm forgetting something.
  How do these stories always start, again?
  Oh! Right.
  I remember now.

Once upon a time...

PROLOGUE

I stare at the stranger in the mirror.
Her wild hair, uncharacteristically coiled.
Her lush mouth, unusually solemn.
Cloaked in sadness the royal jewels cannot disguise.
Wreathed in a destiny she is unequipped to embrace.
She holds a nation's fate within her shaking hands.
She wears a crown that never should've been hers.
A golden lie.
A dirty halo.

♛

YOU KNOW the funny thing about fairy tales? You never see what happens to the pretty scullery maid *after* she rides off into the sunset with a dashing prince in a gold-plated carriage and shacks up in his castle.

Fade to black. Roll credits.

And they lived happily ever after.

Or… did they?

How are we so damn certain the minute that maid steps foot in that unfamiliar fortress, she doesn't realize what a monumental mistake she's made? Why are we so sure the prince doesn't reveal himself to be a total prick once the haze of lust has cleared from her head? What if instead of a happy ending, the pretty maid spends the next thirty-odd years wishing she'd never met her goddamned fairy godmother in the first place?

I know what you're going to say.

But the jewelry! The clothes! The handsome prince with his handsome steed!

Spare me.

I, for one, would rather spend the rest of my days scrubbing floors than find myself stuck in some stuffy castle surrounded by stodgy rich people, forcing a fake smile for six long, flavorless courses.

But nobody asked what I wanted.

Nobody gave me a choice in the matter when they pulled me from my life and dragged my size six, donut-loving ass through the castle gates, into a destiny I thought I'd successfully dodged.

That fairy tale ending?

I'm living it.

And I'm here to tell you…

It fucking sucks.

👑

ONE MONTH EARLIER…

👑

CHAPTER ONE

"THE KING IS DEAD."

The news breaks across the country like an unexpected summer storm — all at once, in a downpour that mutes the whole world with its sudden ferocity. It's one of those moments people will recall with perfect clarity for the rest of their lives, even looking back a half-century later. The millennial generation's very own Challenger explosion or JFK assassination, crystalized forever in a flashbulb memory.

Where were you when you found out about the Lancasters?

The details are so sharp, their edges cut me when I turn them over in my mind. The stale taste of beer on my tongue. The smell of cracked peanut shells, littered across the scratched bar in front of me. The screech of static from the overhead speakers as the recycled playlist of one-hit-wonders cuts off with a violent switch-flip.

Owen presses closer at my side, his broad shoulder warm even through the fabric of his fitted black T-shirt. Voices in the crowd around us grow from a dull murmur to a horrified roar as

3

a sea of liquored eyes turned as one toward the wall-mounted televisions all around the pub. I crane my neck to see what the fuss is about and feel my whole future fragment into pieces.

DEADLY FIRE AT WATERFORD PALACE

Shouts of, "Turn up the volume!" are swiftly traded for gasps and sobs as the images play out onscreen.

Flames and death.

A fairy tale crumbling right before our eyes.

Owen swears under his breath, but I can barely make out the sound. My brainwaves have turned static. My fingers tremble as I set down my beer, feeling dizzy from more than just the alcohol in my veins as I watch the news anchor's lips spout truths I'm unequipped to process.

"The fire caught sometime after ten o'clock this evening in the east wing of Waterford Palace. An inside source informed us that the blaze most likely originated in the crown prince's private suite." Her tone is suffused with shock and grief. "At this time, we can confirm that both His Majesty King Leopold and Queen Consort Abigail have perished in the flames. We do not currently know the status of Crown Prince Henry, but we will update you as soon as we hear whether he is among the dead."

A collective cry splits the air — a lighting strike in this storm of disbelief. The bartender drops a glass with a clatter. Owen lets out another low expletive. The two girls to my left begin to weep. Their horror is so potent, I can taste it on my tongue with each breath.

Feeling strangely removed from my own body, I watch my hand like it belongs to someone else as it reaches out to pass the tearful girl a square bar napkin. She accepts it with a sniffle, her eyes never shifting from the television screens. Looking around, I see her horrified expression mirrored on every other face in the crowd.

It doesn't matter that they've never shaken their king's hand, that they've never seen their prince in person except perhaps from the safety of a sidewalk barricade as his carriage rolled past during a royal parade. This news is a blade plunged into the very fabric of our existence. Even the newscaster is wiping away tears as the grim tale unfolds.

"Whether this was an accident or something more sinister remains unclear," she reads from her teleprompter, looking contradictorily grim in her cheerful yellow blazer. "Authorities are preliminarily treating it as a terror attack and emergency protocols are now in effect: all remaining members of the royal family — including the king's younger brother Prince Linus, Duke of Hightower — have been placed under the protection of the King's Guard and will remain so until the full threat has been assessed."

At the mention of the duke, Owen's eyes find mine in the dimness, an unfamiliar streak of worry in their depths. He's one of the only people on the planet who knows about the paternal name on my birth certificate.

"Emilia…"

"Don't." I pick up my beer glass so I have something to do with my hands. I squeeze so tight, I'm half-surprised it doesn't shatter to pieces as I watch the rest of the broadcast.

"In this darkest hour…" The anchorwoman's voice cracks along with her composure. "I believe I speak for all of us here at GBTV — and every Germanian citizen listening out there — when I say our thoughts and prayers are with every member the Lancaster family as we attempt to navigate this tremendous loss… and what it will mean for the fate of our country…"

"Sweet fuck," Owen murmurs as the screen cuts to more images of the burning inferno. His voice sounds a million miles away — along with the rest of the world. In this moment, surrounded on all sides, I feel even more alone than I did as a little girl, the day my mother finally told me the truth about my biological father. About the man who was almost hers. About the destiny that was almost mine.

He didn't want us, Emilia.

He didn't want you.

Dizzy, I sway into my best friend's chest. He steadies me instantly, his broad hands locking around my bare biceps with reassuring weight. It's warm within the crush of the crowd, but I'm suddenly freezing in my black crop top and fitted skirt. Goosebumps cover every inch of exposed skin.

"Ems?" His brow furrows with concern. A lock of wavy blond hair falls into his worried brown gaze. "You okay?"

I manage to nod. At least, I think I do.

Onscreen, the anchor's hand flies to her ear. "We bring you now to Gerald Simms, the palace press secretary, for an official update."

The broadcast turns to a split-screen. The man that appears on the right side of the television has the sourest expression I've ever seen, as though he's just stuck his nose into a carton of curdled milk. His thinning hair and expanding waistline are not aided by the unflattering pinstripe suit he's chosen to wear for this occasion.

"Mr. Simms, welcome," the news anchor says. "Thank you for taking the time to speak with us tonight."

"Yes, yes." The man's double chin wobbles like a turkey's gobbler. "My pleasure."

"Mr. Simms, can you weigh in on the implications for the crown in the face of this catastrophic loss? Was this a planned attack? Can you give us any insight at all?"

"I can reveal at this time that the King's Guard is actively investigating all leads," Simms says, chest puffing up like a helium balloon. He's so full of self-importance, you could pop him with a pin. "I cannot comment officially on the status of Prince Henry. However, I have been briefed that the king's younger brother

Linus, Duke of Hightower, is safe and secure at an off-site location."

"That's excellent news."

Simms nods. "If his nephew is unable to rule in the immediate future, I'm told he is prepared to take up his mantle as king regent in the interim. And if the prince is killed..." A bolt of unease shoots through the crowd around me at those words. "He will be crowned king as soon as possible."

The newscaster nods sharply. "Please correct me if I am wrong, but while the Duke has two step-children from his marriage to Lady Octavia Thorne, he has no legitimate heirs of his own. Is that accurate?"

The word *legitimate* makes my blood run cold.

"Yes. Quite." Gerald Simms blinks his beady eyes. "At times like this, we are unfortunately reminded why the royal family practiced that *heir-and-a-spare* policy for so many generations." He shakes his head and the extra flesh beneath his chin wags. "If Linus cannot produce an heir, for the first time in history, Germania may find itself without any viable contenders to rule."

"Unbelievable." Owen's handsome features twist into a scowl. "The crown's not even fucking cold and they're putting contingencies into place. *Vultures.*"

My brows lift so high, they nearly disappear into my hairline. "Says the boy who spent his spring semester marching in anti-monarchy protests. I wasn't aware you gave a shit about King Linus or Prince Henry."

His eyes flicker to mine and hold for a long moment. There's something indecipherable in their depths. Something that makes my heart flutter uncomfortably inside my chest as he leans a fraction closer, his voice dropping to a harsh, angry whisper.

"I give a shit about what might happen if that crown changes hands to the king's younger brother. For fuck's sake, I give a shit about what that might—" His teeth sink into his bottom lip. He doesn't say the rest, but it's written all over his face.

Of what that might mean for you, *Emilia.*

I glance away sharply, wishing I could block out the sudden fear coursing through my veins. Wishing I could alter the strands of my DNA as easily as I do the strands of hair on my head. Wishing a lot of useless things.

"I'm sorry, Ems." Owen swallows, his Adam's apple bobbing roughly. "I didn't mean to snap at you."

I bump my shoulder into his to let him know I'm not upset. It would take far more than a few terse words for me to actually be mad at Owen. We've been friends since our alphabetically assigned desks landed us beside one another back in kinder-garten. It's hard to imagine him doing anything that could ever jeopardize our bond. He's the one constant in my life, no matter what else changes.

The talking heads on the television chat for another few moments, trading detestable words like *lineage* and *line of succession,* but I tune them out, trapped deep within my own thoughts. My eyes flit over the graphics that flash onscreen — a royal family tree, King Linus and Queen Abigail already crossed out with resolute black lines. Their small portraits seem to lock eyes with me from the screen, ghostly and grave.

In another life, they would've been my aunt and uncle.

Now, they're a memory.

Feeling numb, I stare at the blank branch on the Lancaster family tree below Linus — the branch where my name should reside — and swallow down the bitterness that rises like bile in the back of my throat. The news anchor zooms in on his face, on the words *DUKE OF HIGHTOWER* scrawled beneath his visage. As my eyes move over his weathered features, I can't help flinching at the striking similarity to my own.

Same dark, thick hair.

Same endless green stare.

Same stubborn set to his full-lipped mouth.

"Who is that?" One of the crying girls in the crowd whispers to her friend, peering at the television through glossy red eyes.

"Haven't you been listening? It's the king's younger brother, Linus. The Duke of Hightower," her friend whispers back. "If the prince dies... he'll rule."

"Isn't he, like, seventy?" her friend asks.

"Seventy three, last month," I murmur without thinking.

Both of them glance at me a bit strangely. I look away before they can question why I'd know such an obscure fact. The onscreen authority is still prattling on, saying things I don't want to hear.

"We will have an update on Crown Prince Henry within the next few moments..."

I go totally still, hardly able to breathe, and send up a prayer to whoever might be listening for the cousin I've never met.

Please survive, Henry.

You have to survive.

You have to rule.

A solemn hush descends over Hennessy's, the nondescript little dive around the corner from campus we frequent on nights when I don't have class and Owen isn't stuck at work. On a Friday night, it's typically ground zero for debauchery. Now, it's eerily silent, with even the drunkest patrons seeming to hold their breath.

Owen's hand settles on my hipbone — heavy and warm, pulling me close. It's an intimate touch; one that might make my brows lift, under normal circumstances. But these circumstances are anything but normal. I can't spare more than a moment to wonder whether my best friend is crossing the unspoken boundary that's been there for as long as I can remember, because the anchor is back, her voice piercing the airwaves with fresh horror.

"Though we still await official confirmation, we are now hearing reports that Crown Prince Henry is alive but unconscious. He has been admitted to the intensive care unit in critical condition, undergoing treatment for third degree burns, smoke inhalation, and severe head trauma. It is not known whether he will survive the night."

The room is so silent, I can hear the rhythmic *drip-drip-drip* of a leaky sink behind the bar. Each droplet sounds like the report of a gun in the stagnant air. The newscaster takes a deep breath and steadies her yellow-blazered shoulders. She stares straight into the camera, her brown eyes unwavering, and delivers a broadcast that will be replayed on a loop for the next hundred years, archived in history museums and national annals until the world fades into dust.

"Several minutes ago, Linus, Duke of Hightower, was officially sworn in as king regent." Her voice goes faint as she recites the official motto of Germania, so quietly it sounds like a prayer. "Non sibi sed patriae."

Not for self, but country.

"God bless King Linus," the anchor says solemnly, practically choking on the customary words. "Long may he reign."

"Long may he reign," the bar-goers around me echo back at the screen, their voices morose and fearful as they stare at the projected image of their new monarch.

King Linus.

My father.

CHAPTER TWO

SUDDENLY, it's all too much.

The press of the crowd, the dull roar of the television, the weight of my unknown future resting sharply on the blades of my shoulders. I can't catch a breath, can't hear anything over the rising tide of panic roaring between my ears.

Owen is saying something to me; I can see his mouth moving, but none of his hushed syllables permeate. I mutter something about needing air and shove out of his grip, beelining for the front exit. He's close on my heels as we cut a path through the dense crowd. No one seems to know where to look or what to say. They are paralyzed, unable to process the news that their kingdom has crumbled, staring dazedly at the televisions as though they're trapped in a nightmare from which they'll wake at any moment.

The bouncer who checks IDs at the front door barely spares me a glance as I barrel out into the crisp October night. I take a few halting strides until I reach the side of the brick building, where an abandoned cobblestone alley offers a modicum of privacy.

I focus on the things I can wrap my spinning mind around. The feel of cool brick pressed against my forehead. The half-moons of my fingernails cutting into my tight-clenched palms. The breath inside my lungs, expanding and emptying, emptying and expanding. An endless vacuum.

After a few moments, I sense Owen's presence at my back. He doesn't touch me, doesn't say a word. He simply stands there, offering silent comfort. Just as he has through every skinned knee and failed grade, bad date and broken heart.

My best friend.

"Ems…"

"I'm fine," I whisper in a choked voice. "Totally fine."

"But—"

"*No!*"

Whirling around to face him, I plant my hands on my hips and fix him with a severe glare. At five-foot-two, I'm hardly an intimidating figure — Owen towers at least a foot above me — but height is the least of my problems if I look even half as ragged on the outside as I feel on the inside. My dyed curls cascade around my shoulders in a messy lavender curtain. My chest heaves against the fitted crop top, exposing a pale sliver of stomach muscle with each labored breath. My mini-skirt is riding high on my thighs, which are tensed from the urge to bolt. My green eyes are a bit too wide, too wild, as they glare up into his.

In other words, I'm a hot mess.

Somehow, he doesn't laugh at me. In fact, as he takes in all my tattered edges, his expression is so solemn, he's damn near unrecognizable.

"Like it or not, Ems… you aren't fine," he says gently. "And how could you be? This is your family."

"No," I repeat, quieter this time.

"You might be able to convince everyone else in that bar that this doesn't affect you. Hell, you might even convince yourself, if you try hard enough." His eyes burn into mine. "But you can't pretend with me. I know you too well."

"I don't want to talk about this anymore, Owen," I say thickly, wondering why the air suddenly feels so heavy. "Those people aren't my family. They never have been. *They never wanted to be.*"

Owen sighs. "Ems…"

"Why should the death of some monarch matter more to me than it does anyone else in that bar? Why should I grieve people who never wanted me?" My voice quivers pathetically but I push onward, determined to get the words out. To expunge them from my body like deadly poison. "Why would I mourn people who threw me and my mom aside like dirt?"

"*Emilia.*"

There's a heartbreaking crack right down the center of his voice. He takes a step toward me, closing a shade of the space separating my body from his. His hand lifts from his side carefully — so achingly carefully — and with a tenderness that makes my breath catch, he cups my face. His callused thumb caresses my cheekbone and I suck in a sharp breath at the foreign sensation that small, simple touch sends spiraling through me.

"Emilia," he repeats lowly, and there's something new in his voice. Something I've never heard before, in all the years I've known him. A mix of determination and desperation and…

Desire?

Frozen in place, all I can do is watch as he shifts toward me, ever so handsome in the pale moonlight. A blond lock of hair falls across his forehead as he leans down to close the full foot of space between our faces. I don't have time to wonder whether the world has turned upside down, whether I'm hallucinating, whether my best friend is about to bring his lips to mine and change everything between us… because before he can close those final few inches…

Screeeeeech!

The jarring squeal of rubber on asphalt fractures the night sky, bringing reality crashing down around us. We spring apart, both our heads whipping toward the sound, and watch as two black SUVs careen up onto the sidewalk in front of Hennessy's.

Instinctively, Owen shoves me behind him, acting as my very own human shield as the mammoth vehicles slam to a halt at the mouth of the alley. Their headlights blind us in a halo so bright, I lift my arm to shield my eyes from the glare. I hear the creak of car doors opening, the swift crunch of boots against cobblestone, but my stinging retinas can make out only silhouettes of the men closing in on us, blocking any chance of escape.

What. The. Fuck.

Owen tries to shove me deeper into the alley, but there's nowhere to go. My back hits a brick wall, far too tall to scale.

Whoever these guys are, they are not fucking around. They move with methodical precision — a highly trained unit, not uttering a single word as they flank us on all sides. There are four of them, dressed in nondescript black suits. Their cold, assessing eyes scan us up and down, even as their peripherals monitor the perimeter for unseen threats. I lose my breath when I see the handguns strapped to their hip holsters.

For a split second, I think they're actually going to kill us in cold blood, our bodies left to rot in this forgotten alleyway like garbage, but they make no moves to take out their weapons. Still, I'd be lying if I said my heart wasn't pounding double-speed inside my chest. And though Owen's shoulders appear steady, I can feel the rapid intake of his breath through the thin fabric of his shirt.

He's scared, too.

I peer around his shoulder, trying to get a better look at the men. They don't offer any identification or explanation for their sudden appearance. As much as I'd like to believe otherwise, I know in the marrow of my bones that they aren't here for Owen.

They're here for me.

My frantic thoughts trip over each other as they fight for position at the forefront of my mind.

But who sent them?

Friend? Foe? Or… god forbid… father?

"Emilia Lancaster," the nearest suit says in a dead voice.

I flinch. I've been going as Emilia Lennox for so long, I almost forgot what the name on my birth certificate says.

Almost.

"We need you to come with us." The man's voice is as empty as his stare. "Immediately."

I try to speak, but I can't get more than a squeak of air past my numb lips.

"Not a fucking chance," Owen growls on my behalf, pressing me tighter against the brick. His back muscles flex with tension. "She's not going anywhere with you."

The suit places a hand on his holster — a clear threat. When he speaks again, his words are punctuated by tiny droplets of spittle as he enunciates each word with lethal clarity.

"Last warning. *Step. Away. From. The. Girl.*"

Owen doesn't move a single inch. "Go. Fuck. Yourself."

The man moves so fast, he's practically a blur. I don't see him pull the gun from his holster, but I do hear the awful thud it makes as it cracks down against Owen's head with enough force to send him staggering off balance. A scream tears out of my throat as I watch my best friend crumple to the cobblestone, his hands pressed over the gaping wound on his temple. Blood flows quickly between his fingers, spattering the stones like red rain.

"*Owen!*"

Two suits step over him like a piece of rubbish and advance

on me. Their companions look on impassively as four iron-clad hands clamp over my biceps. I try to keep my eyes on Owen, try to thrash out of their steely grip as they haul me into the glaring headlight beams like a bug toward a zapper-trap, but it's no use. They're too strong.

Within seconds, I'm manhandled into the backseat, my head shoved down to avoid banging the roof like a criminal being loaded into a cop car. The last thing I hear before the door slams shut behind me is Owen's voice, clogged with pain and panic, ringing out into the night.

"*Emilia!*"

👑

OWEN'S SCREAM echoes in my ears long after we jolt off the sidewalk and race down the street, the engine roaring like a wild thing beneath the hood. I'm alone in the backseat. I can't see much of anything with the partition up, closing me off from the suits in the front.

Attempting not to panic — *oh, who the fuck am I kidding, I'm totally panicking* — I try the door handles, but they're locked tight. Likewise for the dark-tinted windows. I look around for my purse and my cellphone… before realizing I left them sitting on a barstool in Hennessy's, where they're of absolutely no use to me.

Perfect.

My search beneath the seats turns up empty as well. No convenient tire irons left out for me to use as a weapon, no pointy objects I can jam into a bad guy's eyes given the opportunity. I'm officially on my own.

I press my eyes up against the glass, trying to see outward, but there's only darkness as we hurtle through the night to destinations unknown.

"Let me out of here!" I scream, banging my fists against the partition. "Are you insane?! This is kidnapping!"

There's no response from the other side of the wall.

"I'll call the police!"

I cease banging to listen, but there's nothing. Not even the faintest indication they've heard me. The car turns with a sharp screech of tires, and I go flying across the leather seats. My elbow smacks into the glass window with enough force to leave a mark. Blinking tears from my eyes, I rub my funny bone and force myself to fasten my seatbelt. No use dying before they have a chance to murder me.

We drive for about twenty minutes before I feel the brakes engage. When the engine shuts off, I un-click my belt and go perfectly still, waiting for the moment my door will open, waiting for them to drag me out of the SUV to certain death…

A minute passes in silence. Then another. My bare knees bounce up and down with tension as I wait. And wait. And wait. Finally, I hear raised voices outside. Not the suits — I can't imagine them letting their steely composure slip even for an instant — but someone else, yelling incoherently as he's led toward the vehicle, the slurred outrage in his voice growing louder as they approach.

Another captive?

A moment later, my suspicions are confirmed when the opposite door jerks open. I lurch forward, thinking I might squirm my way out, but there's nowhere to go. My exit point is blocked by a wall of brawn in tailored black wool. The useless scream for help dies in my throat. All I can do is watch, stunned, as a boy is shoved into the backseat along with me.

Correction: not a boy.

A man.

A highly inebriated man, judging by the scent of bourbon emanating from his pores. I think my BAC increases, just breathing around him. Or maybe that intoxicated feeling is simply a byproduct of staring at his face because, dear god, even in the dim light of the car I can see how insanely attractive this guy is. I don't know what he's doing here with me, but he looks like he just walked off the set of a movie.

Fifty Shades of Great-Now-My-Panties-Are-Wet.

In his mid to late twenties, he's solid muscle in crisp white button down and charcoal dress pants, with the most chiseled features I've ever seen outside an airbrushed magazine spread or filtered Instagram feed. His eyes are glazed with liquor and lust, ringed by a thick set of lashes any girl would kill for. His cheekbones are so sharp they'd probably cut your heart clean in two if you were ever stupid enough to get too close.

Hell, he might as well be holding up a neon sign that says ABANDON ALL HOPE, YE WHO ENTER HERE. It would be a fairer warning for those poor souls attempting to guard their hearts — and ovaries — around him.

Get it together, Emilia.

Tearing my focus from the striking stranger, I try to catch the eyes of one of our suit-wearing kidnappers. I'm beyond pissed at myself for getting so distracted, I didn't scream for help when I had the chance.

"Wait!" I yell, locking eyes with one of the gun-toting guards. "Please—"

Before I can finish my plea, the suit gives a sharp shove that sends the drunk, dark-haired stranger toppling forward into the SUV — practically onto my lap. I hear the door slam shut behind him and the locks engage, but I don't glance that direction. I'm a bit preoccupied with the messy head of black hair currently face-planted in my crotch.

Seriously, could this night get any worse?

CHAPTER THREE

"GET OFF ME!" I squawk, blinking stupidly at the back of his head.

"I usually buy a woman a drink before she lets me put my head between her thighs," he mutters, his deep voice muffled by the fabric of my mini-skirt. "But if you're game, love…"

Snarling, I roughly shove him off me and smirk with no small amount of satisfaction as his forehead bonks painfully against the partition.

"Fuck!" he curses. "What was that for?"

"You really have to ask?" I mutter, watching warily as he maneuvers his body onto the seat beside mine with a groan. His eyes are pressed closed, so I can't see their color, but I find myself studying the angles of his face in the dark. The set of high cheek-bones protruding beneath his tanned skin. The broad column of his throat, each corded muscle on display with his head craned back against the leather.

"Can I help you with something?"

I flinch. "Excuse me?"

"You're staring."

How did he know?!

I whip my head forward to face the partition, cheeks flaming. "I was not."

A low chuckle assaults my ears. "Whatever you say, Violet."

"*Violet?*" I ask, glancing back at him despite my best intentions.

One eye cracks open — crystalline blue, a whole Caribbean sea in a single iris — to peer over at me. "The purple hair."

Oh. Right.

I reach up to smooth my lavender strands, feeling suddenly self-conscious about my most recent color choice. Last month, I was an ashy gray-blonde. Before that, I was navy blue. I haven't seen my natural hue since I was old enough to do something about it.

"Disguise or distraction?" he asks lowly.

"Excuse me?"

"The hair." His eyes are a shade too perceptive for my liking. "Only one reason a girl who looks like you does something like that: she's hiding — either from herself or someone else."

"You don't know anything about me!"

"True enough." His eyes flicker to my mouth and back. "But I know women."

Before I can think of a clever comeback, the stranger reaches across the space between our seats and grasps a rogue curl between his thumb and his index finger. In a deliberate gesture that makes my heart stutter, he trails his way slowly down the lock, stretching the curl to its full length. When he reaches the end of the strands, his eyes flicker up to mine.

"You know, V…" The smirk returns and, with it, a husky tone that makes my palms sweat. He leans in, as if he's sharing a secret. "I like a little color in my life."

Ignoring my racing heart, I smack his hand away. The curl

springs back upward toward my breasts. "Hands to yourself, bourbon."

"*Bourbon?*"

"Yes. As in, the smell radiating from your pores," I explain sweetly, gesturing at him. "Since we're trading nicknames."

"Touché."

For a frozen instant he just sits there, watching me watch him. His liquor-drenched eyes rake me up and down, taking in every detail at his leisure. I'm not sure if the alcohol has lowered his inhibitions or if this is simply *him*, even sober: a walking, talking sexual proposition.

Probably a little bit of both.

Pushing aside the urge to fidget, I set my face in a dispassionate mask and boldly return his gaze. In my head, I pick him apart piece by piece, hoping I might discover some fatal flaw.

What a useless endeavor.

Even his imperfections are attractive. The bump in his nose suggests he's got a few bar fights under his belt. The small scar bisecting his left eyebrow lends character to a face that would be *too* perfect, in its absence. And if his dark hair is messy, it's only because someone has been running her fingers through it all night — or, so I'd guess, judging by the smudge of bright magenta lipstick marring his collar.

What kind of girl left that pink kiss behind? I can't help wondering. *What kind of girl spent her night with him, her fingers up in that hair, her lips on that muscular throat? What kind of girl would he pick out of a crowd and take home to ruin?*

Probably some model-perfect blonde with killer hair and a knockout figure.

"Do you—" I shake my head, doing my best to banish the thoughts to the back of my mind. "Do you know what we're doing here? Why they grabbed us?"

"*Me?* Yes. *You?* Not so much." His eyes narrow a shade. "Who are you?"

I stiffen. "I'm no one."

"I doubt that."

I try to glance away, but his eyes — those blue, blue, blue eyes — are holding me captive.

"You wouldn't be in this car if you weren't important. So... *who are you?*" he asks again, less patiently. "A friend of Chloe's? Octavia's new assistant? Gerald's long lost niece?"

"What the hell are you're talking about?" I swallow hard, hoping it might dispel some of the panic rising in my chest. "Look, there's been some kind of mistake. I'm not supposed to be here. I don't know any of those people you just rattled off. I'm not important. I'm *no one.*"

He lifts his hands in a defensive gesture and settles back against his seat with a sigh as his eyes slip closed once more. "Suit yourself."

Angling my body away, I cross my arms over my chest and look resolutely out the window. I shouldn't be wasting time talking to him anyway — no matter how gorgeous he is.

You have bigger fish to fry than your sorely-neglected sex life, Emilia, I remind myself. *Or have you forgotten that you've been taken against your will? That they cracked your best friend over the head with a gun and left him bleeding in a dark alley? That, as much as you'd like to deny it, you have a sinking suspicion you know exactly who ordered these men to extract you from your life in an SUV that costs more than your yearly tuition...*

We drive for a little while, only the sound of the road beneath the tires breaking the silence between us. It's so quiet, I can hear each rhythmic breath he takes. He doesn't seem particularly concerned about our situation. In fact, he seems downright relaxed. It's an infuriating contrast to my own state of distress.

"How are you so calm?" I snap after another minute has passed in total silence, glancing back at him despite my best efforts.

22

His eyes don't open.

"Hello? Can you hear me? Or did you hit your head so hard you've slipped into a coma?"

The only indication he's listening is the slight curl of his lips, twisting up in a smirk.

I sigh deeply. "We need to strategize. I think together we might have a shot at taking them down, when the door opens. If we—"

He snorts — *loudly* — and finally opens his eyes. "Are you serious?"

"Of course I'm serious!"

"Love, it's been a long night. A night which I intended to spend getting gloriously drunk to forget about all the shitty things that have happened today. Instead, I'm stuck with a delusional purple-haired pixie who's either legitimately dumb or simply playing it, and, to top it off, my bourbon has run dry. Which means a hangover of massive proportions is soon to hit." He closes his eyes once more. "So, no. I'm not going to *strategize* with you. I'm going to sleep and hopefully, when I wake up, this entire fucking day will have been a nightmare. You included."

Purple-haired pixie?!

Nightmare?!

What a prick.

If he won't fight back, I'll just have to do it alone. With a snarl of disgust, I turn to the partition and begin to wail on it with both fists.

"LET ME OUT OF HERE!"

I bang and bang until my flesh is stinging and sore.

A dozen hits.

Fifty.

One hundred.

"LET! ME! OUT!"

My raw screams are punctuated by skin-tearing strikes. My

muscles are aching with the effort, but I don't stop.

"WHERE ARE YOU TAKING US?"

An angry tear streaks down my cheek. I don't pause to brush it aside.

"YOU FUCKING BASTARDS!"

He moves so fast, I don't even see him coming. One minute I'm pounding the partition, the next I'm pressed tight against a broad chest, my wrists neatly manacled by two massive hands, my ass firmly planted on two unyielding thighs. I try to jerk myself free, but his arms are steel bands. It would take a brick of C4 to extract me from his hold.

When his mouth hits my ear, I go absolutely motionless; I don't even dare draw a breath, frozen like a helpless bird between the paws of a lion.

One wrong move, he could tear me to pieces.

"Enough," he orders in a soft tone that somehow lacks all gentleness — like the whisper of a sharp blade sliding into the space between two ribs. I thrash, but he doesn't release me. In fact, he only pulls me tighter against him, until I can feel every delicious indentation of his chest plastered against the planes of my back. From this proximity, his scent — secondhand smoke and top-shelf bourbon and something spicy I can't quite put my finger on — is intoxicating enough to make my head spin.

"Let go of me," I hiss between clenched teeth.

"I will, when you agree to stop hurting yourself."

"Hurting myself? I'm trying to get us out of this mess."

"Love, there's no getting out."

"You haven't even tried!"

"Thing you should know about me..." His nose grazes the side of my throat and I try not to shiver. "I don't expend effort on useless outcomes. I'd rather put my energy into more... *viable*... pursuits, where the endgame is guaranteed to be satisfying. For all parties involved."

My thighs clench of their own volition. I never thought the word *viable* could be so damn sexy.

I was wrong.

"Listen, buddy," I bark. "*You* may be completely unbothered by the fact that we're trapped in here, about to be sold into the sex trade. Or the internal organ trade. Or... some other kind of illegal back alley trade HBO will no doubt release a documentary about in the coming months..."

He snorts.

I ignore the sound. "But *I* haven't resigned myself to dying before my twenty-first birthday. So let go of me. *Now.*"

"Only twenty," he murmurs, his breath warm on my skin. "So very young. So very naive."

"As opposed to you, hardened and wise in you old age?" I scoff bitterly. "What are you, twenty-five? Twenty-six?"

"Too old for you, in any case."

"Perfect, since I'd never in a million years be interested," I hiss scathingly. "Now let me go. I mean it."

"Or what?" The streak of humor in his tone tells me he's enjoying this verbal sparring.

I clench my jaw. "I'll... I'll..."

"Scream at the top of your lungs? Bang your tiny little fists raw?" He chuckles again, and I fight the urge to head-butt him. "Because that plan has been working *so* well for you. "

"You're an asshole."

"You don't even know me."

"Thank god for small miracles," I snap. "Now let me go."

"In a minute. When you're calm."

I thrash again, but it's a halfhearted attempt. All I manage to do is land myself more firmly in his lap. Realizing there's only one way out of this, I expel a sharp breath and strive to slow my rapid pulse.

Breathe, Emilia. Just breathe.

For the next few moments, we simply sit there — two strangers pressed together in the dark, his body cradling mine like a steel glove — as I attempt to calm myself. Instead, my heartbeat, which by all accounts should be slowing, begins to speed. The tempo of my breath increases, faster and faster, in time with each warm exhale I feel against my neck. Without any conscious effort at all, my spine bows slightly against his chest. I feel his thigh muscles flex beneath me and an unbidden bolt of arousal shoots straight between my legs.

Fuck.

The currents in the air change, one sort of tension fading into another so swiftly, I can't quite define the moment I stop feeling like a captive in his hands. So subtly, I can't pinpoint the second his hold alters from one of confinement to...

Something entirely different.

I hear a sharp intake of air from him, and I know he feels it too. His fingers flex against the thin bones in my wrists, as though he's fighting for control. Not over me — I've long since stopped struggling. Over himself.

"Tell me your name," he mutters, shattering the silence. There's a new edge of need in his voice that wasn't there before. "Tell me who you are."

A reckless part of me wants to whisper something crazy — *I'll be whoever you want me to be* — just to see how he'd react. To throw down a challenge and watch him rise to meet it.

"I already told you," I force myself to say instead. "I'm no one."

With a low sound of frustration rattling his throat, he shifts against me, in the process bringing my ass into full contact with the seam of his pants... and the undeniably swollen shaft that's sprung to attention beneath. We both freeze at the impact.

Holy.

Fuck.

He's huge. And hard as a rock.

It takes all my strength to hold my spine rigid, to keep my muscles tensed with indifference when every atom in my body is screaming that I should do the exact opposite. My heart is beating so hard, I'm sure he can hear it pounding at the pulse-point in my neck.

Honestly, I hate that a man I've never met before is affecting me this much, this fast. I hate that he's been nothing but a jerk to me and, still, there's a sudden throb of desire in my veins that I can't ignore.

Hate it.

Hate this.

Hate him.

So… what does it say about me that I'm more turned on than I've ever been in my life?

"Please," I murmur. I'm trying to say *please let me go* but I can't seem to conjure the rest of the words. For some unfathomable reason… my plea comes out sounding like I'm pleading for a wholly *different* sort of release.

"Please what, love?"

I sink my teeth into my lip to contain the sound of pleasure that bubbles up from a dark, dangerous place inside me I don't want to acknowledge. A place that would gladly let this stranger take anything he wanted from me in this dark backseat, while giving me what would probably be the most exciting sex of my boring, vanilla life.

What the hell is the matter with you, Emilia?

"You were right, you know." His lips find my ear again and I practically moan at the sensation of his warm breath on the sensitive lobe. "I *am* an asshole. You'd be wise to remember that."

Before I have a chance to retort, he releases me. Face aflame with shame at my own weakness, I scramble off his lap, back to my side, as far from him as I can manage in this confined space.

It's no use — even pressed up against the hard plastic door panel, I can still feel his hands on my wrists, his breath on my neck, his heat pressing into my back, his cock pulsing between the cheeks of my ass. Every atom in my body is buzzing with supercharged sexual energy.

And I don't even know his name.

Even without looking at him, I know he's watching me. The weight of his stare rubs my nerve endings raw. I hope he can't see the stained red skin of my cheeks in the dark: evidence of just how thoroughly he managed to work his way beneath my skin in a few brief moments.

In *theory*, I'm smart enough to know that men like this are nothing but trouble — maybe served up with a side of a few screaming orgasms, but trouble all the same. Unfortunately, in *reality*, it's a lot harder to ignore the ache spreading through my bloodstream like a lethal dose of heroin.

"Stop looking at me like that," I whisper, eyes dead ahead.

There's a heavy pause. "Like what?"

"Like you're trying to guess what color my underwear is."

"Love, I don't need to guess. That skirt is so short, all I'd have to do was lean forward to find out."

My eyes roll so hard, I'm surprised they don't get lodged in the back of my skull. "Of all the people I could've gotten abducted with, of course I end up with someone like you…"

"I'll take that as a compliment."

"You *really* shouldn't." I scoff, exasperated. "Apparently the horror of being grabbed by beefy men in bad suits and shoved into an SUV like a scene out of a bad James Bond movie wasn't traumatizing enough. The true torture is an hour-long car ride in the company of an unbearable alpha male with a chip on his shoulder the size of the royal treasury."

"You know, that's not the only thing the size of the royal treasury…"

"You're revolting."

"Funny, that's not the vibe I was picking up from you while you were writhing in my lap."

"You mean when you sexually harassed me without consent?"

The air goes so still, so tense, I almost cave and glance over at him. Clearly, I've struck some kind of nerve, because when he speaks again all teasing has been stripped from his voice. It's almost a growl.

"I only grabbed you because you were hurting yourself, like a child having a tantrum. What happened after that, the way you reacted to me — that was something else. If you want to twist it in your head, if you want to pretend you didn't feel it, that's your prerogative. But don't cry assault when we both know your racing pulse and wet panties are evidence of something else."

I flush, chastised by his cold words.

Great job, Emilia. Twenty minutes in his presence, he already hates you.

I open my mouth to apologize, but promptly snap it back closed. What could I possibly say to fix this? And why would I even bother?

He isn't my friend. He isn't my ally. He's just a stranger in a bad situation.

Probably safer to keep it that way.

The SUV rolls on beneath us, a steady rumble over unknown road. And though nearly another hour passes, we don't speak again. Not when we feel the car make a sharp left turn. Not when we slow to a stop. Not even when the suits yank open the back doors and haul us out into the night.

We're finally here.

....wherever that may be.

CHAPTER FOUR

I'M NOT sure what I was expecting.

Some kind of secret Germanian government facility? A wartime bunker complete with semi-automatic weaponry and helicopters circling overhead?

Instead, I find myself teetering in my chunky black heels on the uneven gravel lining the circular driveway of a stately manor-house in the middle of the countryside. It's three stories of impressive baroque architecture with a mansard roof and a marble-arched front doorway. There must be twenty windows on each floor, inset at precise intervals along the thick stone facade, all illuminated brightly from within.

It's not a castle, but it's damn impressive.

I'm so awestruck, I don't remember why I'm here until a crunch of gravel beside me pulls my attention back to earth. My dark-haired stranger stands a handful of feet away, his tone dripping with disdain as he surveys the scene.

"Seriously? The Lockwood Estate?" he scoffs, eyeing the nearest guard. "The extraction protocols demand you bring me somewhere *safe* — not somewhere so far removed from anything remotely interesting, I'll want to blow my own brains out after thirty minutes."

The suits, predictably, don't react except to start walking toward the front door. It's clear we're expected to follow, but neither of us makes a move. I, for one, am in no rush to find out what awaits me across that threshold.

Or... who awaits me.

I let my eyes slide over to the man at my side. He's taller than I thought in the car — well over six feet — and he seems determined not to meet my gaze, staring at the house like it's the first ring of hell, rather than a stunningly beautiful mansion. Belatedly, it occurs to me that he himself might be royalty. His presence alone means he's connected to the Lancasters. I just really hope I'm not expected to call him *my liege* or *my lord* or some other pretentious title... because that will *not* be happening.

For the first time in my life, I curse myself for forcibly ignoring everything about the royal family. For avoiding news channels, looking away from tabloid magazine covers, tuning out idle chitchat about the dashing prince with the girls in my freshman year dormitory. I always told myself I had no interest in wasting brain cells on such frivolity, but the truth is... it was too painful to be an outsider pressed up the glass, peering in on a life that was almost mine.

And, now...

Here I am.

I glance at my stranger again. My mouth opens to ask him a question, but I snap it closed before a single word escapes. After our intense tête-à-tête tete back in the car, I'm not sure we're still on speaking terms.

He expels a sharp breath. "For fuck's sake, just ask."

I blink, startled. "*What?*"

He looks down at me like I'm the most annoying person to

ever dare breathe his air. His dark brows are pulled into a scowl that somehow only makes him more handsome. Or maybe that's the moon's doing. Out here, in the middle of nowhere, far removed from any source of light pollution, the starlight is so bright it bathes his every feature in pale, monochrome perfection.

"Now or never, shrinking violet."

"Where are we?" I ask before he can change his mind.

"The Lockwood Estate."

"Yes, but *where* is that?"

"About a quarter league past bum-fuck nowhere."

I sigh. "Thanks. That's immensely helpful."

He shrugs unapologetically, shoving his hands into the pockets of his perfectly tailored gray dress pants. "This place is about halfway between Lund and Vasgaard, if memory serves."

"Why are we here?"

"I assume you saw the news earlier."

"The fire?"

"Yes." A bolt of grief flashes through his eyes, buried away so fast I'm sure I imagined it. "When there's a threat to the crown, the whole royal family is put on lockdown, along with their closest relatives, friends, pertinent connections... You get the idea."

I nod.

His eyes narrow on me. "Since you never told me who the hell you are, I'm assuming you're connected to someone of importance. Someone who wanted to ensure your safety, in case this fire turns out to be..." He runs a hand through his hair, his jaw clenching with sudden strain. "Something more than an accidental candle left burning in Henry's chambers."

The casualness with which he refers to the crown prince strikes me instantly.

Henry.

They're close. Friends. Maybe even family.

I suddenly remember his earlier words.

It's been a long night. A night which I intended to spend getting gloriously drunk to forget about all the shitty things that have happened today.

I feel myself go pale. God, I've been so wrapped up in the chaos of my own night, I didn't realize he might have his own fair share to deal with.

"I'm so sorry," I say quietly, tamping down the urge to reach out and take his hand in mine.

He recoils as though I've slapped him. "*Excuse me?*"

"The fire... the king and queen... Prince Henry..." My voice goes soft. "I'm sorry for your loss. For what you must be going through, right now."

His eyes hold mine for a long moment. I might as well be staring at two cerulean shields — he's totally unreadable. I should probably look away, but I don't. The space between us starts to simmer again, strange currents charging the air. When he finally breaks the silence, there's gravel in his voice.

"You done?"

"*Done?*"

"With your questions."

"Not nearly."

"Too bad." He looks away sharply. "Time to face the firing squad."

I must make a sound of distress, because his smirk returns.

"The metaphorical firing squad." He pauses. "Then again, when Octavia sees that hair of yours..."

"Who's Octavia?" I squeak, but he's already walking toward the guards, who are waiting for us at the steps leading up to the front door. "Who are you? Who's in there? *Wait!*"

"Sorry, love. The Q&A portion of the evening is over."

"But you've barely told me anything!"

"Next time, ask better questions."

I let out a grumble. I have no choice but to scamper after

him, tugging down my mini-skirt and smoothing my hair as best I can as we round the edge of an ornate fountain surrounded by elaborate topiary. My heartbeat increases in direct proportion to our dwindling distance from the doorway. By the time we ascend the five marble steps to the threshold, four guards flanking us from all sides, I'm sure I'm about to keel over from a massive coronary incident.

Just before we step inside, two blue eyes cut to mine. "Ready for this?"

"Not remotely," I whisper.

"Last chance to run."

"Thing to know about me?" I steady my shoulders, turn my face forward, and watch as the door swings inward. "I don't run."

With that vow hanging in the air, I step forward into the manor.

♛

In all my life, I've never felt more frizzy and frazzled than I do as my eyes sweep around the Lockwood Estate's soaring atrium. Between the grand staircase, the crystal chandelier, and the carefully appointed collection of antiques, I'm about as out of place as Maria arriving at the Von Trapp family home in *The Sound of Music* — one of the old Hollywood films I used to watch on repeat as a little girl, back when I still believed in happily-ever-afters and fairy tale endings.

There's a rotund man in a pinstripe suit waiting for us. I startle when I realize I saw him on television earlier: the palace press secretary. Offscreen, his expression is equally sour — perhaps more so, when he catches sight of me. His eyes scan from my outgrown lavender roots down to my chunky black heels and back. I know, from that two second perusal, he has taken my measure and found me sadly lacking.

"Well, then," he says in a haughty tone, as though we're inexcusably late for an appointment. His jowls quiver with displeasure as he turns his gaze on my companion, evaluating every flaw from the lipstick stained collar to the messy hair to the bloodshot eyes. "Lord Thorne, you may go occupy yourself doing… whatever it is you do in your vast free time. Just do not leave the premises."

"How magnanimous, Simms," my stranger — *Lord Thorne?* — drawls from beside me. "But I think I'll stay for the show."

"If you wish, my lord." Simms sighs tiredly before his eyes slide back to me. "As for you…"

My brows lift.

He pivots sharply and starts walking down a hallway to the left. "Follow me, please."

I glance over and find Lord Thorne — *I am never calling him that aloud, I don't care if it's a royal transgression* — watching me carefully.

"Still don't want to run?"

"Nope," I lie through clenched teeth.

He smirks, as if he knows I'm full of shit, and gives a mocking bow. "After you, then."

I swallow hard, set my shoulders, and stride after Simms, trying not to wobble on my heels. God forbid I stumble into a 15th century antique end table and break it. I may be petite, but I've never been exactly graceful. Mom always says I move through life like a force of nature, a tornado overturning everything in my path.

Always said.

The verb tense still trips me up, every now and then. It's been nearly two years, but I'm still not used to her being *past* instead of *present*. I doubt I ever will be.

We pass several closed doorways as we move to the end of the hall, where an archway opens into a large sitting room. I press my lips together to keep my jaw from going slack with awe.

Everything is decorated in creamy tones, from the furniture to the curtains to the pale hardwood floors beneath my feet. Tasteful bookshelves line the walls, a grand piano dominates one corner, and three white settees are artfully arranged around the focal point of the room — an incredible marble fireplace, its mantelpiece thicker than my body and twice as long.

The only point of color in the room is the coiled auburn hair of a glamorous middle-aged woman sitting by the roaring fire, her legs crossed gracefully, the white linen of her dress a perfect match for the settee beneath her. When my eyes meet her light blue ones, I try not to flinch at the icy unwelcome in her stare. Thankfully, they soon move past me to focus on the man at my side.

"*Carter.*"

It's truly amazing how much distaste she's able to convey, just saying his name — a name that, it must be said, suits him well. *Lord Carter Thorne.* I glance at him and find his whole demeanor has changed. He's carrying himself differently: his shoulders stiffer, all traces of humor and nonchalance stripped from his countenance. He might be made of the same marble as that fireplace, for all the humanity left in him.

"Where is Chloe?" the woman asks in that same frigid tone.

"I'm not her keeper, Octavia."

The woman doesn't react, other than to reach out and lift her teacup off the coffee table in front of her in a smooth, soundless move. She takes a methodical sip, holding Carter's eyes the entire time over the rim in some sort of strange staring contest. I'm not sure who they are to each other but the air between them is so frosty, I'm surprised I can't see my breath. Even Simms looks uncomfortable as he hovers dutifully by the far wall, awaiting a command like a well-trained dog.

Carter breaks eye contact first, glancing down at his dress shoes. I'm standing close enough to hear the resigned exhale of air that hisses out from his lips. "Last I heard, Chloe was going to a club opening in Lund with Ava. I'm sure they went straight to the hospital when they heard the news about Henry."

The woman sets down her cup and saucer without even the faintest rattle before lifting her eyes back to Carter's. "And you didn't feel you should accompany them?"

"To sit there and watch him die? No. I think there are enough people doing that already."

"You're being quite dramatic."

"And you're being predictably indifferent." Carter's voice is a snarl of disgust. "God, Octavia, you could at least pretend to feel a little grief for Henry. But why bother, right? You've landed yourself exactly where you've always wanted to be. I expect you'll be doing cartwheels down the castle corridors, as soon as the smoke clears."

"Again with your dramatics." Her lip curls with disdain. "Someone has to step up in this time of turmoil, to take command before things begin to spiral out of control. Though, seeing as you live your life stumbling belligerently between one party and the next, I wouldn't expect you to understand what I'm talking about."

"War profiteering?" he suggests bitterly.

"*Duty*." Her blue eyes flash. "I will step into the role that has been thrust upon me and do what I must for the sake of my family, my husband, and my country."

There's a marked pause before Carter's hands begin to smack together in slow, mocking applause. I flinch with each sharp clap in the silent room. In the corner, I see Simms doing the same.

"Wow." Carter whistles. "That was a nice little speech. Almost sounded *rehearsed*. Something you've been practicing *for weeks*."

"Rehearsed?" The redhead's voice drops low. "Don't be absurd. This was a terrible accident."

"If it was such an *accident*, why have we been quarantined here under full guard?" He shakes his head. "We both know this was something more. An attack."

"That remains to be seen. Perhaps Chloe will provide more information when she arrives. " Her eyes scan him up and down. "At least one of you is of some use."

"Oh, mother, do stop — you'll spoil me."

Mother?!

She continues to stare coldly at Carter. "You expect my praise? You look as though you've just stumbled out of a brothel."

"Maybe I have," he seethes, jaw clenched tight. "But that shouldn't be a surprise to you. Chickens always come home to roost — isn't that right, Octavia?"

I'm not sure what, exactly, he means by that, but its evident *she* does. The words are an undeniable blow. She goes pale and her manicured fingers clasp so tight, I can see the whites of her knuckles even from here. The way she's looking at her son, she'd clearly like nothing more than to cross the room and slap him across the face. Instead, in an eerie show of composure, all she does is smile placidly.

Who the hell are these people?

Thoroughly uncomfortable, I shift from foot to foot, wishing I could teleport myself literally anywhere else in the world to escape the suffocating malice of this room. Instantly, I realize my mistake — the small motion draws Octavia's laser-like attention to me. Her eyes flicker up and down, practically dripping with hauteur as she takes in my scanty clothing, my limp curls, my smeared eye makeup.

"And here I thought you were joking about the brothel." She

shakes her head. "Did you truly think it wise to bring one of the escorts here with you?"

Wait, what?!

"Hasn't this family endured enough for one night?" Octavia hisses. "Why must you insist on always making a scene?"

A low, angry sound rattles in Carter's throat. "Octavia—"

"Honesty, I am so very tired of these attention-seeking stunts! Your stepfather—"

"Excuse me," I cut her off, stepping forward before she can spout another venomous word. She looks completely dumb-founded that I — *a common brothel wench!* — have dared interrupt her diatribe. "Did you just call me a prostitute?"

She sniffs, as though she smells something foul, and doesn't deign to answer.

"Perfect!" I snap, my hands flailing out in a burst of pent-up emotion. "Just fucking perfect. That's the goddamned cherry on top of the goddamned cake!"

There's a simultaneous gasp from Simms and Octavia at my crass language, but I'm too worked up to stop myself, let alone apologize. "You people send armed guards after me, have my best friend bludgeoned over the head, throw me in the backseat of an SUV with absolutely no explanation, drive me to the middle of the countryside…" My voice crescendoes with each word. "And now you actually have the gall to sit there and CALL ME A WHORE?!"

As though she hasn't heard a single word, Octavia reaches out and picks up her teacup again. Her eyes scan me up and down once more — the rapid rise and fall of my chest, my hands planted on my hips, my furious glare — and with a delicate sniff she takes another infuriatingly slow sip of tea.

Ugh!

I take a threatening step her way but jolt to a stop when a warm male hand lands firmly on my shoulder. *Carter.* His fingers flex against my bare skin, but I'm not sure whether it's to comfort me after my outburst or warn me against continuing it.

"You two are quite the melodramatic pair, aren't you," Octavia says haughtily. "Feel free to tell us who you are and why you are here." When I don't respond, her eyes flicker to the press secretary. "*Gerald*! Who is this girl? Why is she here, privy to our private family matters?"

Simms' double chin bobs nervously. "Your Grace... She... Well..."

"Spit it out, Gerald."

Simms has gone beet red. "She's... she's..."

"She is my daughter," a deep, rasping voice says from the doorway.

Octavia's teacup crashes to the carpet with a clatter.

Carter's hand disappears from my shoulder.

Simms lets loose a chortle of pure distress.

And I — well, I don't do a damn thing. I can't. I'm frozen with dread and fear and rage.

No.

It can't be.

Heart in my throat, I force my feet to pivot around toward the archway. My trepidatious gaze lifts to the man standing within it. His thick, salt-and-pepper hair has just the slightest hint of wave. His skin is weathered with sun and age. His eyes, the deepest shade of green, hold neither warmth nor recognition.

And why would they?

We've never met. We're nothing to one another.

He didn't want us, Emilia, Mom's memory whispers. *He didn't want you.*

For a full minute, there is total silence in the parlor. I don't think anyone dares to breathe — not Carter, not his mother, not Simms, not the three suited guards flanking the man with whom I share strands of DNA. Least of all me.

Linus takes two strides into the room, that evaluative stare unwavering as he takes me in — purple hair, exposed midriff, bared thighs, brazen expression.

If he's shocked by my appearance, he doesn't let it show. Not that I'd give a fuck if he found me lacking. I stopped waiting for his approval around the same time I gave up playing dolls and dress up.

My chin jerks higher, so he knows I'm not intimidated. Maybe I'm supposed to bow my head in supplication, maybe I'm supposed to play nice — *he is the king, after all* — but I can't bring myself to show even an ounce of respect to the man who threw me and Mom away like the condom he should've been wearing the night I was conceived.

Bastard.

Oh, wait. No. That's *me*.

His green gaze sweeps around to address everyone in the room and, in a voice that rings with kingly authority, he says the words that alter the entire course of my life.

"Her name is Emilia Victoria Lancaster. She is my daughter. And, as it currently stands… she is next in line for the throne. The Crown Princess of Germania, by blood and by right."

CHAPTER FIVE

"No," I whisper, reeling backward at his words.

I bump straight into the hard wall of Carter's chest. It takes all my strength not to lean into him. To let him absorb the weight of my watery bones, now that my knees have gone weak. The room tilts around me as those words spin through my mind.

Next in line for the throne.

Crown Princess of Germania.

He must be mad — that's the only explanation. I'm not the only one who thinks so, either.

"Linus!" Octavia is out of her seat and across the room so fast, I'm not confident she doesn't posses powers of teleportation. "Tell me it's not true."

"I'm afraid I can't," Linus says, never shifting his eyes from mine.

God, he looks like me. Or, I suppose, *I* look like *him*. And I hate it. Hate it so much, it makes me want to smash every mirror in the world, to have my face surgically altered, to burn every picture I've ever taken in a sacrificial fire.

"But you *cannot* be serious!" Her shrill tone pierces my ears like a knife. "Look at her! She can't possibly be—"

He stiffens. "She is my daughter, Octavia."

"Perhaps we should discuss this matter in *private*," she says pointedly. "Before any hasty decisions are made—"

"Hasty?" His brows lift skyward. "This is not an act of haste. If anything, it is twenty years overdue."

"But—"

"My decision is final. I will not hear another word on the subject."

Octavia's lips press into a thin line. Her eyes slide to me and I'm grateful that looks cannot, in fact, kill people because otherwise my blood would be spattered all over their immaculate white oriental rug.

"Your Majesty," Simms interjects in a placating tone, breaking the stilted silence. He bows slightly at the waist, formally greeting his new king. "If I can be of assistance in any way at all, please let me know. Whether drafting a statement for the press or helping with smaller matters. I am at your disposal."

"Thank you, Gerald. If you would please ensure that there are suitable rooms ready for Emilia's use upstairs. And perhaps send for appropriate ensembles. We won't be briefing the press quite yet — not until Emilia is..." His eyes flash back to me. "Settled in."

Read: made to look like a properly groomed princess.

I roll my eyes.

"Of course, Your Majesty. I will contact the palace personal shoppers immediately and have them send a selection of clothing first thing in the morning." Simms glances at me. "Your size, miss?"

I cross my arms over my chest instead of answering. I refuse to be party to my own reinvention.

"Very well." He bows shallowly to Linus again before he

43

turns and walks out of the room, muttering to himself. "Trial and error it shall be…"

Silence descends again. Octavia uses the opportunity for one final plea.

"Linus…" Her eyes dart quickly to me. "Are you certain she is…*yours*? Have you had the necessary testing done to prove—"

"*Octavia.*" The steel in his tone is sharper than a broadsword. "This is not up for discussion. "

"So, you expect me to… to… to simply take her into our *home*?" Her perfectly waxed brows furrow. "To allow her to live alongside us, as though she is a part of this family?"

"I would expect you to take in my child, as I once took in both of yours." Linus glances at Carter, who's hovering a few feet to my left, then back to me. "I apologize, Emilia, you must be terribly confused. Allow me to formally introduce my family. This is my wife, Octavia."

"A pleasure," the redhead lies thinly. Her smile involves neither teeth nor joy.

I go still.

His wife.

But that means…

When I don't say a word, Linus hurries on. "And I believe you have already met my stepson, Carter." He gestures to my left. "He's your stepbrother, now, I suppose."

My stepbrother.

I try to nod, but I can't. I'm paralyzed. Carter seems equally so, though I don't dare look his direction.

"The guards informed me you were both in Vasgaard when the extraction protocols went into effect." Linus nods his approval. "I hope you had the chance to bond a bit, during your trip here."

Oh, we bonded all right.

My head turns slowly to the left, dread saturating my every

molecule. My eyes tangle with Carter's as soon as I glance up. He's guarded as ever — a locked box of emotion. The only clue he's feeling anything at all is the rhythmic ticking of tension in his locked jaw, the tight clench of his hands into fists at his sides. Horror washes through me in a potent wave as I remember the feeling of those hands on my skin, not so very long ago.

A dark backseat.

A silent spark of desire.

The ache between my thighs.

The hardness beneath his seam.

My near undoing.

My new sibling.

Nausea coursing through me, it takes all my composure to keep from vomiting on the carpet at my feet. I break eye contact with him, unable to meet his stare for another second. I've never been claustrophobic, but I suddenly feel as though the whole world might cave in around me.

I have to get out of here.

I have to run.

Back to my life.

Back to reality.

Octavia and Linus have begun sniping at one another, but none of their words hold any real weight.

"What would you suggest instead, Octavia?" Linus sighs. "I am too old to father children, and you're too old to carry them."

"There are other ways!" Her voice is insistent. "A surrogate, or—"

"*No.* If Henry doesn't recover, the line of succession is clear. Emilia is the heir apparent."

I shake my head, rejecting those words, but he's not even looking at me as he plots out my entire future — regardless of whether or not *I* want any part of his grand plans.

"The people will be looking to the crown for strength, right now. We cannot afford to appear crippled by the loss of my brother. We need to give them something to hold onto. A new ruler to throw their support behind." He nods to himself, eyes far-seeing. "They will rally behind her. The Lancaster line will be restored in the eyes of the world."

"Linus, I understand that, but she's——" Octavia breaks off in distress. "This girl is…"

I arch one brow, waiting.

Octavia's nose lifts haughtily. "She is in no way equipped to represent Germania on a grand-scale."

"Nevertheless, she must," Linus counters. "And, someday, when I die, whether you like it or not, my dear… she will inherit. She will rule."

"Like hell I will," I interject, finally finding my voice.

Every head in the room turns in my direction. For a minute, no one says a word.

"*Excuse me?*" the king growls.

"I have no interest in…" I gesture vaguely at my surround-ings. "Any of this. I don't want your name or your birthright. I have no interest in becoming a… a…" I can't bring myself to utter the word *princess* aloud. It's far too absurd. "A Lancaster," I finish lamely.

"Your interest is irrelevant," Linus thunders, rage clouding his expression. "This is your destiny. Your responsibility."

"You have the audacity to speak to me about responsibility?" I choke out. "That's rich, considering you felt approximately *zero* responsibility for me until about three hours ago when, as far as I can tell, your precious monarchy suddenly found itself short a few viable heirs to the throne."

"You have no idea what you're talking about." Linus looks like he's about to blow a gasket. "Clearly, your upbringing has been sorely lacking in discipline, manners, and credible information. Don't worry — we will strive to compensate for every gap in your education your mother did not see fit to fill."

I go stock still.

Did he just say what I think he said?

Leaning forward, I make sure to articulate clearly, so he can't possibly dismiss my next words as an idle threat. "I don't care who you are or what titles you go by. If you ever insult my mother or her parenting again, make no mistake —*you will live to regret it.*"

All three guards step forward, hands on their holsters. Carter edges closer to me, worry in his eyes. For good reason. To insult the king is bad enough... but to openly threaten him?

That's courting treason.

Octavia presses a hand to her heart, aghast at my impropriety. "You dare speak to your king in such a manner, girl?"

"Oh, I dare," I hiss, already moving toward the door. "Now, if we're done here... I think I'll get back to my life."

"You would turn your back on your crown?" Linus yells after me. "On your country?"

"As far as I'm concerned, you can take your royal legacy and shove it up your ass." With that, I dart out the archway, down the hallway, and through the front doors, into the night.

♛

FORTY MINUTES LATER, I'm still pissed off, but anger has taken a backseat to a more pressing sensation: *cold*. Shivering, I rub my bare arms with fingers that have long since gone numb. My knees bounce, a futile attempt to generate some much-needed body heat. It's no use — I'm damn near hypothermic, every inch of exposed flesh covered in goosebumps.

The stone bench I found in the side garden seemed like an ideal spot when I first stumbled upon it, steam still leaking from my ears after the scene inside. But now, after nearly an hour, my bones are aching, my lips have chapped, and each freezing gulp of air burns its way down my throat like fire. To top matters off, it begins to rain — a stinging, spitting drizzle that pelts my face and quickly soaks me to the bone.

"Perfect," I mutter to myself, watching my breath puff in a small cloud.

It's unseasonably chilly for October, even this high up in the mountains. I realize I'll have to go back inside eventually — it's that or freeze to death out here, seeing as my attempt to hijack a vehicle was unsuccessful. When I stormed out of the manor, I was greeted by the uncompromising stares of the same four bulky guards who grabbed me earlier — members of the elite King's Guard, I realize now, tasked with protecting the Lancasters.

Which, apparently, now means me.

Emilia Victoria Lancaster.

The Crown Princess of Germania, by blood and by right.

I wince.

Much as I'd like to pretend this is all one big cosmic joke, I know better. Linus — I can't bring myself to call him anything else, even in my head — is deadly serious. He intends for me to be named publicly as the heir apparent. Acknowledged in front of the entire world as his child.

How's that for irony?

I mean... it's every bastard's dream. Isn't it? To be claimed. Legitimized. To have the parent who never wanted you sweep suddenly back into your life and tell you it was all a terrible mistake. That they're sorry. That things will be different, from this point onward.

Hell, it was *my* dream, once upon a time.

But not anymore.

Because I know now that dreams come with strings attached.

As Mom used to say: *when something seems too good to be true... that's usually because it is.*

A shiver rattles my teeth. God, it's freezing. The lure of warmth and shelter inside the manor is growing harder to resist, the longer I'm perched out here on this sodden bench. I wipe rain out of my eyes and glance longingly at the Lockwood Estate.

Two of my guards stand in the shadow of the great house, silhouetted by the light pouring out the first story windows. Keeping watch on me, despite the steadily-increasing downpour. They haven't tried to force me inside yet, but I know it's only a matter of time. They're bound by oath to protect me — even from my own pigheaded decisions.

"I have to say," a wry voice comments from the shadows, scaring me half to death. "This isn't the best plan I've ever seen."

Whipping my head around, I suck in a sharp breath when I see Carter standing there in the rain, his white dress shirt plastered against his muscular chest like a second skin. *Sweet Christ.* It should be criminal for someone to look that hot while sopping wet. Especially when that someone is your new stepbrother.

"Wh-what?"

"This." He shrugs. "You, dying of exposure to avoid becoming the princess. It'll work, sure, but I think there must be an easier way."

I try to laugh, but it comes out sounding suspiciously like a sob instead. "Right, well, let me know if you think of one, because I've been out here racking my brain and so far I'm coming up empty."

"I don't know about you, but I brainstorm a hell of a lot more effectively when I'm warm. Dry. Preferably with a glass of bourbon in my hand." He hesitates a beat, then takes a step forward and extends his hand. "Come on."

I don't move except to tilt my head questioningly. "I thought you were supposed to be an asshole."

"I am."

"Could've fooled me. In my general experience, assholes don't brave the elements to help some — what was it you called me, earlier?" My lips twist. "Oh, I remember. Some *delusional, purple-haired pixie* you barely know."

"Fine." He snatches back his hand. "Forget it. Freeze to death, for all I care."

Grumbling to himself, he exits down one of the garden paths and disappears between two rose bushes in the space of a few strides. Before I have time to talk myself out of it, I'm on my feet, racing after him.

"Wait!" I call breathlessly, nearly slipping on the slick stone path as I careen around a prickly shrub. "Wait, Carter I was just messing with— *oomph!*"

I careen into his chest hard enough to knock the wind from my lungs. He grunts in pain, rocking backward to absorb the impact. His hands automatically close on my biceps, steadying me against him. My hands find his sides, clinging for purchase in the damp fabric of his shirt.

"Christ!" he curses.

"I'm sorry!" I gasp. "Really, I didn't mean to—"

"For such a tiny person, you cause a remarkable amount of fallout."

The apologetic words poised on my tongue never make it out. Instead, a burst of uncontrollable laughter bubbles up from my stomach and explodes out my mouth. Carter blinks down at me, his dark brows pulling together with concern. For some reason, that only makes me laugh harder.

Deep down, I know nothing about this day is even remotely amusing. But right now, I feel delirious enough not to give a damn that I look like a crazy person, cackling in the rain.

In my stepbrother's arms.

The ridiculous thought inspires a fresh fit of giggles. I try to stop, but I can't. Tears of mirth — *or are they real tears, after all?* — mix with the rain on my face. Carter's fingers flex against the flesh of my arms, but I barely feel it. I'm floating outside my body, lighter than air, lighter than wind, lighter than the weight of crushing responsibility on my shoulders. So light, I'd float away if he were to let me go — up, up, up to the stars where there are no words like *birthright* or *destiny* or *succession* to push me down.

"Hey! *Hey.*" He gives me a light shake. "Emilia."

It's the first time he's ever used my name and it moves through me like a bolt of electricity. My laugher evaporates as suddenly as it appeared, leaving behind a hollow ache that would scare me, if I could feel anything at all.

"Emilia?"

"I'm okay," I whisper in a voice I hardly recognize as my own. "I'll be okay."

"God, your skin is like ice." He rubs my arms. "We need to get you inside."

"I don't want to go back in there, yet."

"Too fucking bad!"

"Please," I whisper. "Don't make me go back in there. Please, Carter…"

He sucks in a sharp breath. His eyes blaze in the darkness, thoughts I'm afraid to decipher swimming in their depths. And I know it's wrong… but right now, I'm feeling weak enough that it doesn't seem to matter. Winding my arms around his back, I lean into him and soak in his heat.

His strength.

He tenses, but I only hold him tighter — clinging like he's my life-ring in rough waters, like he's the only thing keeping my head above the waves of exhaustion crashing through my system.

After a moment, I feel his chin come down to rest on the top of my head. After another, his arms slide cautiously around my back. He holds me like he's out of practice — as though the simple act of an embrace is so far removed from his normal realm, he's not sure how to proceed. I'd actually feel sorry for him, if I had a single ounce of emotion leftover to spare for anyone else.

Absurd as it seems, for a long time we stand there in the pouring rain, arms wrapped around each other. It's not sexual. It's one human reaching out in need of comfort, another grabbing hold and offering it.

Or maybe that's just what I tell myself.

I try not to think about the scent of his skin… the sound of his breaths over the patter of the rain… the contour of his chest muscles beneath my cheek… the fact that, if I turned my face up to his, our mouths would be only a few scant inches apart…

Let go.

Step back.

Move away.

I ignore my own advice far too easily. Sucking in a sharp breath, I tilt my head backward to look up at him. His eyes meet mine instantly — blue, blue, blue, and full of questions I can't answer. From this close, I can make out the thin rings of navy around the edge of each iris.

"Thank you," I whisper, wishing my voice wasn't trembling.

He doesn't respond — doesn't react at all except to lift one hand and slowly push a plastered lock of hair out of my eyes. The rain continues to fall in a steady torrent, spattering both our faces. I stare at the droplets clinging to his lashes, watch how he winks them away like tears, and ignore the part of me that longs to taste them as they race down his cheeks.

"Carter, I… I…"

A low sound rattles in the back of his throat as he leans in, closing a tiny fraction of the space between us. For a single instant, I think he's going to do something utterly reckless…

Instead, he drops his arms and pulls away.

"We should go," he says flatly, shoving his hands into his pockets, looking anywhere but at me. "They'll be looking for us."

"Right. Of course." I clasp my pruned fingers tightly together as I turn my back to him, heading down the path that leads back to the house as fast as my legs can carry me.

Ten minutes ago, I would've rather stayed out here all night than stepped foot in that manor again. Now, the Lockwood Estate looks pretty damn good, compared to the prospect of even one more minute spent bonding with my new *brother*.

CHAPTER SIX

THIS HOUSE IS HAUNTED.

If not by actual dead spirits, then by the ghostlike guards and service staff who move silently down its many halls, only the vaguest creak of floorboards giving away their presence. Maybe I'm being paranoid, but I can't shake the sensation that there are eyes on me at any given moment.

Watching.

Waiting.

As we stand in a semi-dark hallway upstairs, I shift anxiously from foot to foot while Carter roots through a linen closet in search of towels. My legs, still aching from our ascent up that endless grand staircase, drip steadily until a small puddle forms on the hardwood beneath my feet.

"Here."

It's the first world he's spoken to me since our walk back from the gardens. It might as well be a scream in the eerily silent house. I shiver and glance around. There are too many rooms with locked doors, too many creeping shadows, too many strangers lurking just out of sight.

"*Here*," Carter repeats impatiently, shaking the towel in his grip.

I grab it and wrap the warm fabric around my waterlogged crop-top and skirt, which are clinging like a second skin. Carter retrieves a second towel for himself before kicking the linen closet closed. The bang of the door in its frame makes me jump about a foot in the air.

"Relax," he mutters, voice muffled by the towel as he pats his face dry. "By now, Octavia is riding the Ambien Express and, though Linus may be the king, the guy could sleep through a damned revolution. He wouldn't wake up until they had him strapped down to the guillotine."

"That must've come in handy as a teenager, when you tried to sneak out of Hightower at night," I murmur, wringing water out of my hair.

His brows go up. "Never had to sneak. The Lancasters aren't exactly proponents of hands-on parenting, as you'll soon find out."

"Oh?" My numb fingers being to tingle as circulation returns. "You assume I'm staying."

"Aren't you?"

"Why would I?"

He simply stares at me.

"I can't just snap my fingers and become... *royal*." I wince at the word. "I don't understand a damned thing about this life."

"Take it from someone who grew up living it — it's mostly boring state dinners and the occasional ribbon cutting or charity event. Smile. Wave. Keep your mouth shut." He shrugs. "Seems to me, they aren't looking for you to be a leader. They need someone to prop up as evidence that the Lancaster line is alive and well, someone they can use to convince the public they're unbroken by the loss of King Leopold and Queen Abigail." His eyes narrow on mine. "Right now, you happen to be pretty much the only person left on the planet who can solve that particular problem. I don't see them letting you walk away from that. Like it or not... you're the vital pawn in this particular game of chess."

"You don't think I know that?" I scoff angrily. "You don't think I realize that the only reason I'm standing in this hallway talking to you right now is because they literally have *no other options* at their disposal?" My voice jumps an octave. *"Don't look now, they've dragged the illegitimate love child out of the shadows!* Really scraping the bottom of the barrel, aren't they!"

"That's not what I meant."

"But it's the truth." I shake my head. "Do you have any idea what it's like to spend your entire life wanting validation from someone, then finally get it... but for absolutely all the wrong reasons?"

His expression turns to granite. *"No.* I fucking don't."

Right. I suppose he wouldn't — not with Octavia for a mother. She doesn't exactly seem like the validating type.

My mouth opens, then promptly closes again. There's little point even trying to make him see things from my perspective. *Lord Carter Thorne* was raised in this life of excessive riches and grand responsibilities. He couldn't possibly understand how strange it is to someone like me — an ordinary girl, thrown gracelessly into a game with rules no one's even bothered to explain.

I glance at the door to the room Simms had the house staff prepare for me. There's a card-stock placard affixed inside the embedded nameplate, etched with my ridiculous new title in sloping calligraphy.

Her Royal Highness Emilia Victoria Lancaster

"Frankly, all of this is a moot point anyway," I say after a long moment, looking sharply away from the door. "Because Prince

Henry is going to recover. He'll take back the crown, he'll rule…
and I'll go back to my life."

"Are you really so eager to return to it?" Carter asks, staring
at me like I'm a puzzle he can't figure out. "Most girls would be
over the damn moon if someone told them they got to live in a
castle and wear a crown. It's the dream, isn't it?"

"Not *my* dream." I pull the towel off my shoulders fold it in
my hands. "I have obligations back in Vasgaard. I can't just
abandon them because some outdated figurehead snaps his
fingers and demands I give up my life, my internship, my spot at
university. Not to mention, there are people I care about—"
Owen's face flashes in my mind and guilt floods me. I haven't
even called him yet; he must be out of his mind with worry. "I
can't just leave him." I finish softly, shaking my head.

Carter's eyes sharpen to blades, cutting into me with each
pass they make over my face. "Poor little princess, can't see her
boyfriend because they've made her royal. *Spare me.* That's not a
real problem, and you know it. You're just looking for reasons to
walk away from something that terrifies you."

I flinch at his callous words. "Back to being an asshole,
I see."

"Fitting, since you're back to being delusional."

I glare at him. "Why do you even give a shit about any
of this?"

"I don't."

"Could've fooled me!"

"Then you're more deluded than I thought."

We glare at each other, both panting. I'm not exactly sure
when this conversation escalated to an argument, but I'm
suddenly flush with anger. From the looks of it, so is he. The foot
of space between our faces practically shimmers with heat, the
molecules bending like air around a boiling kettle.

"If you truly feel that way," I say through clenched teeth.

"I'm *shocked* you didn't leave me out in the rain to freeze to death!"

"Already have one funeral to attend this week," he seethes, hands curling into fists at his sides. "Wasn't in the mood to work another into my social calendar."

"*Wow.*" I twist the towel in my hands, so I have something to do besides wring his neck. "You know, I thought maybe we could be friends. I see now that was a terrible mistake."

"And *I* thought maybe you wouldn't turn out to be an utter pain in the ass. Guess even my instincts are wrong, occasionally."

"Ugh!" The towel falls to the floor, but I barely notice as I take a furious stride in his direction. "You know, of all the awful people I've encountered during this long, miserable day, I have to tell you — *you* are the worst." My voice shakes with rage. "And, just to be clear, your competition includes a father who abandoned me at birth and the evil shrew he married afterward!"

Carter's eyes burn bright with anger but his tone is tightly leashed when finally he speaks again. "I think we're about done with this failed attempt at friendship. Don't you, *sis?*"

"Oh, we're more than done," I snap. "We never even started!"

"*Perfect.*"

Whirling away from him, I stomp to my door and shove my way inside. I start to slam it shut, but make the mistake of glancing across the hall first. My hand stills when I catch sight of Carter standing in his own doorway, directly across from mine — white-knuckled grip on the knob, face dark with fury as he glares back at me.

I know I should shut the door on him, cut off this venom-laced eye contact before things escalate further, but there's a cluster of words still stuck in my throat. I can't draw a proper breath until they're clear.

"You might not be capable of giving a shit about anyone

except yourself, but *I* am. I care about people. It doesn't make me weak for not wanting to leave them behind. "

His tone is so cold, it's barely recognizable. "Anything else?"

"No."

"Good."

Neither of us moves. For the life of me, I can't explain why.

"And I never said I had a boyfriend!" I add angrily, for reasons I decide it's best not to examine too closely.

"Never asked, princess," he fires back, equally hostile.

"Fine!"

"*Fine.*"

My door slams shut a second before his, so hard it rattles in the frame.

♔

Sopping wet and spitting mad, I pace around my prison cell.

Okay, so, it's not a prison cell. It's a bedroom. A beautiful bedroom, actually, done up in pale blue tones, with a massive four-poster bed, an antique armoire, and a merry fireplace. The wood has burned almost all the way down to embers, so I toss in another log and stoke the flames higher, holding my hands near the grate until I finally start to feel warm again.

I search the room for a telephone, but find nothing. For a minute, I contemplate extending my search downstairs but I'm so exhausted, I doubt I'd make it back up that massive staircase. Plus, there's the small fact that I couldn't call Owen even if I did locate a phone: his number is stored conveniently in my cellphone contact list, not my longterm memory.

Technology giveth, technology taketh away.

In the adjoining bathroom, I gasp when I catch sight of my reflection in the mirror over the pedestal sink. I look downright frightening — my mascara streaked into raccoon-like circles, half

59

my lipstick chewed off, my hair a wet tangle of lavender waves. Removing the chunky black heels I never want to look at again, let alone walk in, I peel off my outfit and drop it to the tile floor with a splat. Two minutes later, I sink into the soaking tub with a moan so loud, I worry Carter can hear it clear across the hall.

Not that I care what he thinks.

Asshole.

I close my eyes, slip beneath the water, and let out the scream that's been pent up inside me for the past few hours, building like a tempest from the first moment a yellow-blazered news anchor spoke the words, *"The king is dead."* A burst of bubbles shoots upward, tapering off when I run out of air. Gasping, I resurface, feeling only marginally better.

God, I wish Owen were here.

Not *here* as in *sitting in this bathtub with me.* Just... here. By my side.

He'd know exactly what to say, the precise way to put a smile on my face. He'd make me laugh, even when I felt like crying. He'd be supportive and funny and unafraid to throw his arms around me in a breath-stealing bear hug. He'd put me at ease in an impossible situation.

Unlike certain other individuals who seem a little too fond of antagonizing me whenever the opportunity presents itself.

I push aside images of dark hair and a smirking mouth in favor of blond waves and an easy grin.

Some of the girls in my clinical psychology program find it strange that my best friend is a straight, single guy — who, admittedly, is rather easy on the eyes. When they ask why we aren't dating, I usually shrug and change the subject as quickly as possible.

He's my best friend, I tell them, over and over. *It's just never been that way between the two of us.*

They roll their eyes and sigh at me, like I'm crazy enough to be one of our patients.

Sure, Emilia. Whatever you say.

Over the years, I've had other fleeting friendships — my freshman year dorm mates, the girls in my upper-level classes, a few internship colleagues I'll grab casual drinks with after a shift, every so often. But none of those bonds have ventured much deeper than the superficial smalltalk stage. Honestly, they're more like acquaintances when I compare them to Owen, who's been privy to my every private thought and embarrassing moment for almost as far back as I can remember.

He was there in fifth year when the school bully, Lillian Pillsner, smashed my diorama into pieces right before my big presentation. He was there our final year of high school when Markus Goldstein, my date to the prom, stood me up. He was there two years ago, when Mom went into the hospital with acute pneumonia… just as he was there when she didn't come out again, seventeen days later.

Tears spring to my eyes when I think of Mom. She'd hate this — me, here in this house, here with these people. She disliked the monarchy almost as much as the patriarchy, and spent my formative years lecturing me on the many downfalls of absolute power, concentrated wealth, and a whole other bevy of social issues I could hardly wrap my still-developing brain around. I can still hear her melodic voice, crystal clear even after all this time.

'Limitless power is far more likely to corrupt a pure heart than mend a dark one.'

I'm pretty sure she had me reciting that along with my nursery rhymes.

'Excess breeds selfishness, Emilia. When one is born with nothing, there is nothing he will not give to help another succeed; when one is born with everything, he will do everything he can to keep it for himself.'

A tear rolls down my cheek, hitting the water's surface with a tiny splash.

'I love you, pure heart.'

'Stay bold.'

As I float, I let her words lull me into a state of such calm, I nearly fall asleep. My eyelids are heavy as anvils, but I force them open long enough to scrub away the grime of the day with a small bar of rose soap. I'm not crazy about the heavy floral scent, but it's better than nothing.

By the time I finish conditioning the worst of the snarls out of my hair, the water has grown cold and I'm so exhausted, I'm in danger of passing out right there in the bathtub. I flip a lever and watch the water start to swirl down the drain in a mesmerizing vortex, not moving until the last drops disappear with a low gurgle.

Maybe, in the harsh light of day, things won't feel so dire, I lie to myself as I force myself to my feet. Grabbing a plush bath towel off the heated rack to my left, I wrap myself up in it like a butterfly's cocoon. I'm sure there's a hairdryer lurking in one of the many bathroom drawers, but I'm far too tired to bother — even knowing I'll wake up in the morning looking like I've been electrocuted.

Dropping my towel by the edge of the bed, I collapse face first on the plush feather mattress and worm my way beneath the covers with still-damp limbs. I'm asleep as soon as my eyes close, blessedly too tired to replay all the awful events that have unfolded today. Too tired even to dream about the future and the vast uncertainty it holds.

CHAPTER SEVEN

"So, you're the royal bastard, huh?"

The question jolts me out of a sound sleep. Approximately two seconds later, the weight of a body landing on my mattress bounces me several inches into the air. With a squawk of distress, my eyes spring open and I take in the sight of an unfamiliar auburn-haired girl around my age, sitting at the end of my bed. Her legs are folded up in front of her like a pretzel — knees to her chest, hands on her knees, chin on her hands...

Eyes on me.

"What..." I shake my head to clear it, hoping she might disappear. "Who..."

"I'm Chloe Thorne. Sister to Carter, spawn of Octavia, all around pain in the Lancaster family's ass." Her head tilts. "Nice boobs, by the way."

Startled, I drop my gaze down to my chest and feel my cheeks flame. I completely forgot I fell asleep naked, after my bath. Yanking the sheet up to cover the goods with as much decorum as I can muster, I grit my teeth in the vague approximation of a smile.

"Care to tell me what you're doing in my bedroom at the ass crack of dawn, Chloe Thorne?"

"I hate to break it to you, but it's nearly one in the afternoon."

"What?!"

She nods. "Yep. Had yourself a real nooner. Not that I blame you. Yesterday was a bit of a shock, I'd imagine — some recovery time is probably par for the course."

I run a hand through my wild hair. As I predicted, it feels like I lost a bet involving an an electrical outlet and a fork. "You didn't answer my question."

"I was curious about you. Secret love child, and all. Who would've thought old Linus had it in him?"

"News sure travels fast around here," I mutter.

"Faster than gossip in a high school cafeteria. Plus, I had an inside scoop." Her lips twitch. "My brother. I believe you've met."

"Unfortunately, yes."

She snorts. "Yeah, he mentioned the two of you didn't exactly hit it off."

A bolt of annoyance shoots through my chest. "Mmm. You could say that."

"He's really not so bad," Chloe assures me.

"Uh huh."

"You've had about two hours with him as your so-called brother. I've had twenty-two years. Trust my judgment on this one, okay? His bark is worse than his bite." Her expression falls a bit. "This wasn't an easy family to grow up in."

"So, you're saying it's actually *lucky* I was cast out on my ass like an unwanted piece of rubbish for two full decades..." I nod my head, lips twitching. "Good to know."

Grinning, she reaches into the pocket of her fitted white blazer. I watch as she pulls out a silver lighter and a tightly-rolled blunt, clamps one end between her lips, and lights up.

"You don't mind, do you?" she asks, already blowing smoke out the corner of her mouth.

"Actually—"

"*Great!*" She winks. "There are enough prudes in this house already."

I sigh deeply.

I need coffee. And clothing.

Not necessarily in that order.

"I mean it." Chloe takes another deep hit, closing her eyes as the marijuana's effects begin to roll through her system. "I've only been here three bloody hours. If I get one more lecture about leaving ashes on all this priceless furniture…"

"Maybe they're a bit sensitive about you *starting a fire*," I murmur, my tone sharper than intended. "You know, since a whole wing of the castle burned down yesterday, and all."

She blinks at me, stunned, before barking out a surprised laugh. "Damn, girl. That was *seriously dark*. I think I like you already."

"Great. Now, get out so I can put on some clothes."

She laughs again, clearly not offended by my dismissal, and slides off the bed. I think she's leaving, but she merely crosses to the armchair in the corner where a large white shopping bag rests.

"Here." She tosses it onto the bed. I do my best to catch it one-handed without dropping my sheet. "That was sitting in front of your door when I got here. Compliments of the palace's fleet of personal shoppers. I'm sure they've stocked you with an array of utterly boring outfits. Whatever you do, don't let them select your dress for the funeral — unless you're a fan of something black and boxy, likely with a modest boatneck. God *forbid* anyone in this family ever show a hint of cleavage!"

"When is the funeral?"

"Sunday."

"*Tomorrow?*"

She snorts. "Of course not. A week from tomorrow. Royal functions take eons to plan — especially funerals. And this won't be just any funeral. We're mourning the loss of our king and queen. Before the actual ceremony, the bodies will lie in state for a full week."

My brows lift in confusion at the unfamiliar term.

"They'll be displayed for public viewing at Windsor Abbey," she explains slowly, as though she's talking to a child.

"Sounds rather… morbid."

She plunks herself down in the armchair with a sigh. "It's done so the common people have a chance to pay their respects. Only the aristocracy is invited to the actual funeral."

A frown pulls my lips down. "That doesn't seem fair."

"*Fair?*" She scoffs. "You really are new to this, aren't you?"

I ignore her. "How many are expected to attend?"

"Half the kingdom, from the looks of it. I swear, there's already a queue forming down the streets surrounding the cathedral, and the official vigil doesn't even begin until tomorrow. I saw several groups pitching camping tents, so they wouldn't lose their spots in line."

"That's madness."

"That's *mourning*. You should see it out there. It's like the zombie apocalypse. The whole country's at a standstill. Streets deserted, companies closed, people home from work… Every shop shuttered tight, every flag at half mast. Huge crowds camped out in front of the hospital, praying for Henry. We almost couldn't get the SUV out the front gates this morning."

"How—" I hardly dare ask. "How is he?"

"Alive. Barely." Her face closes down. "I was out last night with his fiancé, Ava Sterling, when we saw the news trending on Twitter. Imagine that? Finding out the man you're supposed to marry was nearly burned alive from strangers on the internet." She barks out a bitter laugh. "Some fucking world we live in."

"I'm sorry. That's terrible."

She nods. "We went straight to the hospital. Spent the night waiting for news, until the doctors ordered us to go home and get some sleep."

I pull in a breath. "So… is he…"

"Dying?" She takes another long hit. Tendrils of smoke curl upward toward the coffered ceiling panels. "That's the billion dollar question, isn't it? Unfortunately, I don't even think the doctors know the answer, at this point. He hasn't woken up. He might never wake up. And even if he does… between the risk of infection from the burns, the damage to his lungs and heart from the smoke inhalation, and the blow to his head that knocked him unconscious… it's highly possible he won't ever be the same Henry we knew before."

My mouth goes dry. I try to speak, but I can't seem to find any words.

Chloe's brows pull in. "Meanwhile, everyone is just sitting home watching the news in a state of panic. I thought the press conference Simms gave this morning would calm things down, but…"

My heart starts to pound. "Press conference? What press conference? What did he say?"

"You really don't know a damn thing, do you?" she asks, amused.

"Did he…"

"Did he talk about you?" Her eyes roll. "No. Not a word. As far as I know, the press hasn't caught wind of you yet."

A whoosh of relief moves through me.

I'm safe.

For now, at least.

One glance at Chloe — now sprawled horizontally in my chair with her feet hooked over one of the arms, designer heels dangling in the air — tells me she doesn't plan on vacating anytime soon. Resigned to my audience, I dig through the shopping bag until I locate a plain white cotton shirt. I grimace at the unflattering neckline when I pull it from the bag.

"What'd I tell you?" Chloe giggles helplessly. "*Boatneck.*"

It may be ugly, but it's better than being naked. I yank it on and rummage through the rest of the clothes until a pair of dressy navy capri pants materialize. They're like nothing I own — far too formal to wear to classes or the clinic. I promptly realize *why* when my eyes snag on the price tag.

"Sweet Christ," I mutter. "What are they stitched with, solid gold thread?"

"One of the perks of princess-hood," she drawls. "The clothes rock."

"Glad to hear there are at least a few perks."

"Considerably more than a few." She flicks the tip of her blunt and I watch a small shower of ashes scatter across the immaculate rug. "As soon as the world knows you exist, designers are going to be tripping over themselves to dress you. Play your cards right, you'll have the power to become a style icon."

"Dreams do come true," I snap sarcastically.

Her eyes narrow, despite the haze of drugs clouding them. "You know, for someone who just had the world handed to her, you're kind of a wet blanket."

"Gee, thanks."

"Yeah, well, if you're looking for someone to throw you a pity party, you've come to the wrong girl."

"I'm not looking for pity. And *you* came to *me*, if I recall."

"Not the point."

"Do you *have* a point?"

Her lips twist. "I can give you all the advice in the world, when it comes to surviving in this place… but you'll get it straight up, no filter. And if we're going to be friends, I'll expect the same in return."

"Fine. You want honesty?" I shove the shopping bag off my bed with the sweep of an arm, smiling as it thunks to the floor. "Excuse me if I'm not overjoyed about my new reality as *Emilia Lancaster: Style Icon.*" I scoff. "I want more from life than expensive clothing and boring state dinners and… and…"

"Modest boatnecks?"

"*Exactly.*"

"So, ask for it."

I blink at her slowly. "What?"

"Ask. For. It." She pushes to her feet and looks at me like I'm the stupidest person she's ever met — an expression that instantly reminds me of her brother. "You're the fucking princess. You've been elevated to a position most of us can only ever dream of possessing, just because Linus happened to blow a load in your mom a few decades back."

I wince. "Was that visual necessary?"

"Probably not." She stubs her blunt out in the flower arrangement sitting on my dressing table and props one hip against it. "Right now, with Henry hanging by a thread and the whole damn country in turmoil… they need you a hell of a lot more than you need them. That's called *leverage*, E. That's called *power.* Stop whining and use it."

I look at her, reeling as her words rattle around inside my head.

She's kind of a genius.

"I thought my fairy godmother was supposed to have wings

and a wand," I say finally, smiling despite myself. "Instead I get a foul-mouthed stoner in designer heels?"

"Yeah, well, I thought when my mom became queen I'd finally get a proper royal title," she volleys back, spritzing herself with a bottle of the perfume on the vanity to cover the smell of pot. "Instead I'm handed an evil stepsister with perky tits and purple hair."

I laugh. "Haven't you heard? Life isn't fair."

Fluffing her long auburn hair, she crosses to the door and yanks it open. "Who fed you that line of bullshit?" she asks, brows arching upward. "Screw *fair*. Life is a chess game, E. Welcome to the board. I suggest you choose your moves carefully."

With one last wink, she slips out into the hall. I barely have time to yell a belated *thank you* before the door clicks closed behind her. And for the first time in twenty-four hours, a smile spreads across my face as I realize that the life I want is still well within my grasp. I just have to be brave enough to reach out and take it back.

That's called leverage, E.

Let's see if my fairy godmother was right.

AN HOUR LATER, all signs of my smile are long gone. I glare at the portly man blocking my path into the private study, his double chin quivering with righteous indignation as he peers down his nose at me.

"I'm sorry, Your Highness, that's simply not possible."

"I haven't been coronated yet, Simms. Stop calling me *Your Highness*," I snap. "And get out of my way."

"King Linus is currently occupied. Official crown business."

"Yeah. You said that." I tilt my head at him. "Thing is, I still need to see him. Urgently."

"He is a very busy man, Your High—" He hiccups when he sees my lethal glare, and wisely changes course. "—Miss Emilia."

"Too busy to speak to his only daughter?" I ask, desperate enough to play any card in my deck, if it means getting what I want.

Simms shifts uncomfortably, but does not yield. "Unfortunately, I cannot make any exceptions."

Crossing my arms over my chest, I try to evaluate him like he's one of the patients at the clinic; try to assess him as one of my professors would, during a practical lesson.

Snappy dresser, suggesting a dramatic streak... Unfailingly loyal to the Lancasters, almost as a point of pride... Aspirations of a long career connected to the royal family...

Between his perfectionist tendencies and the near pathological degree of self-importance, the one potential chink in his armor is that it's not in his nature to burn a bridge with someone who might help further his position, down the line.

Someone like me.

I just have to remind him of that fact.

"You mean to tell me, the king is too busy to speak to the *sole heir of Germania?*"

"I'm sorry... but..." Simms wavers.

"You know, Gerald — can I call you Gerald?" I lean in, eyes locked on his beady brown ones. "I'm new to all of this, so forgive me if I'm off base here... but if I were in your position, I wouldn't want to make an enemy of a girl who might, one day, inherit that *official crown business* they're discussing behind those doors. And as your princess..." My jaw sets in a sweet smile. "Maybe even as your future *queen*... I suggest you let me pass."

His face pales a shade. "This is highly unprecedented..."

I lift my brows and wait.

Approximately three seconds later, he pivots on his shiny shoes and knocks quietly on the study doors. "Your Royal Majesty? Please forgive the impertinence…"

My smile returns.

Leverage, indeed.

CHAPTER EIGHT

I sit in a leather chair staring across a massive mahogany desk, engaged in a staring contest I fear I cannot win with the father I wish I'd never met. It's almost like looking into my own eyes — same deep green shade, same slightly almond shape, same mix of curiosity and caution projected in their depths as we evaluate one another.

It's just the two of us; he dismissed his counselors and his personal guard detail when he saw me hovering in the doorway to his study, Simms chortling out apologies at my side. In the crushing silence left behind, I find myself wishing they'd stayed. I'm suddenly second-guessing my whole rationale for insisting upon this meeting.

"So." Linus steeples his hands in front of him and leans back in his leather chair. "You wanted to see me."

I nod.

"I must say, I'm surprised — given your reaction last night."

My eyes press closed as I recall my outburst. I can't bring myself to apologize, but I do arrange my features into a suitably contrary expression. "Last night, I was overwhelmed and exhausted. It was… a lot to take in all at once."

"Still, I thought you'd be halfway to Hawthorne by now."

I jolt, startled when he names the small neighborhood in Vasgaard that I call home.

"Are you surprised I know where you grew up, Emilia?" he asks softly. "Would you be surprised to learn I know a great deal about you and the life you've led?"

I wouldn't touch that question with a ten-foot pole. The potential answer is far too scary.

My pulse kicks up a gear. "Honestly? I'm more surprised you'd let me go home at all."

"You are not a prisoner, Emilia. You were brought to Lockwood Estate as a form of protection during an emergency. And, despite what you might think, everyone in this household is thrilled to have you here."

"Oh, that's *precisely* the impression I got from the armed guards who dragged me here against my will." I snort. "And *especially* from your wife."

"Admittedly, some are struggling with this transition more that others." A glimmer of humor appears in his eyes. "But even Octavia will come around eventually."

I stare at him skeptically.

"If I may ask… what is it you came here for?" He coughs — a wet, racking sound that reminds me of my mother before she went into the hospital. I try to focus on the talking points I put together, but it's a struggle.

Is he sick?

"Emilia?" Linus prompts. "Much as I enjoy your company, I do have matters to attend to. If you won't tell me why you're here—"

"A negotiation," I blurt.

"Oh?" His expression turns curious. "And what are we nego-tiating?"

"You want something from me — *need* something, actually," I correct rather clumsily, wishing my words were coming out the way I rehearsed earlier in my bathroom mirror. "But I'm going to need some things in exchange."

His bushy gray brows lift. "Do go on."

"I…" I force out the words. "I will agree to *consider* becoming your heir — and I mean really, truly consider it, with an open mind, withholding all judgment — but I can't do that if the whole world is watching me. I want the chance to see what this life would be like without being under the public microscope." My cheeks stain red. "No royal announcement. No press. No pressure."

He doesn't react.

I suck in a fortifying gulp of oxygen and keep going. "This way, you can teach me about the kingdom, about this life, about the responsibilities that come along with being a royal, before I'm locked in for all eternity. *If* you manage to convince me to stay, I will accept my role as the crown princess. But, if not… you will allow me to return to my life, under no obligation to ever take on a royal title." I shrug lightly. "Call it… a trial period."

Surprisingly, he doesn't laugh at me. He simply inclines his head and asks, "And how long would this *trial period* last?"

"Um…" Shit, I hadn't considered that. "A year?"

" Until my official coronation," he counters, his expression unreadable. "In one month."

"But that's not nearly enough time! How can I possibly—"

"This is a negotiation, is it not?" he cuts me off in a stern voice.

"…yes."

"And you are familiar with the meaning of that word, correct?"

I fight the urge to stick out my tongue at him like a child and murmur, "A compromise between parties with opposing interests."

"Exactly right. However, in this case, *my* interests are time sensitive." He sits back in his chair and steeples his hands once more. "One month — during which time your identity will be kept in strictest confidence from all outside the immediate royal family, household staff, and security detail. You will be at my disposal for public events, posing as a new royal aide or some other suitable alias. You will also take mandatory lessons in foreign affairs, traditional dance, and proper etiquette from a tutor of my choosing."

"You've got to be kidding me," I snap, outraged. "You want me to take *princess lessons*!?"

"Twice a day."

"That's absurd!" I jolt to my feet. "I will not be subjected to the humiliation of parading around a ballroom, learning how to flirt and finger-wave like some tiara-wearing airhead."

"Then I suppose you won't be getting whatever it is you so desperately want." He shrugs lightly, as if he doesn't care which path I choose, but his eyes remain intent. "What *is* it you want, Emilia? I imagine something of vast importance, if you're willing to even temporarily take on a role you so clearly despise in order to get it."

Don't let anger cloud your judgment.

Focus on your endgame.

Focus on getting home.

I sink slowly back into my seat and take a deep breath. "I still think one month isn't nearly enough time."

He doesn't say a word.

"But I will concede to it," I agree, wincing at the idea. "*If* you give me what I want in return."

"Which is?"

I swallow hard. "Firstly, I want my belongings returned to me, including my cellphone, so I can call the friend I was with last night and make sure he is okay. I'd also like to see him in person — *today*, if possible. "

"This would be..." He glances down at a folder on his desk. "Mr. Owen Harding?"

A jolt moves through me. "Yes. How did you know that? Is he all right?"

"I assure you, he's perfectly well. So well, in fact, that he's been calling the palace nonstop since you were extracted last night, demanding to speak with you."

"*What?*"

Linus nods. "Quite a determined fellow."

I run a hand through my hair. "He must be going out of his mind with worry..."

"We will, of course, make arrangements for your boyfriend to come here — after he's been screened for potential security threats."

"He's not a security threat! And he's not my boyfriend."

"My mistake." Those bushy brows quirk upward again. "It's simply rare to see such devotion from a... friend."

"Maybe *you* need new friends."

His eyes gleam. "Now that we've settled the matter of Mr. Harding... I assume you have more items on your list of demands?"

"Right." I straighten my shoulders. "My internship."

"At Vasgaard University's Center for Clinical Psychology."

Again, I startle at his thorough knowledge of my life. "Yes."

"A prestigious program."

"Exactly. I worked hard to earn my spot there, and I won't allow all of this—" I gesture around vaguely. "— to jeopardize it, especially when I'm this close to completing my degree. During this trial, I'll need to continue my courses."

"That's not possible."

I stiffen. "Just like that? No discussion?"

He nods. "Just like that."

"So I have to take princess lessons and give up my real ones?" I scoff. "I thought this was a negotiation!"

"To a certain point. However, we cannot guarantee your safety while you are wandering around a university campus."

"No one even knows who I am," I point out. "I'm not in danger."

"We don't know that for sure. We don't have any definitive information yet about how the fire started; however, my head of security believes foul play was a factor. This is not yet public knowledge, but… someone hit Henry over the head *before* the flames spread, and left him in his chambers to die. Which means this was no accident. It was an attack. It was *murder*."

My eyes widen. I'd suspected that might be a possibility, but hearing it confirmed is still a punch to the gut. Linus suddenly looks every bit his age, all seventy three years of life weighing down on him like an anvil.

"My brother is dead. My sister-in-law is dead. My nephew is lying in a hospital bed, clinging to life. This is not the time for taking undue risks, Emilia."

"I understand that," I murmur. "However—"

"*No.* My answer is final. Until we know whether this is an active threat, who the perpetrators are, and whether any other members of this family are targets, extra precautions must be taken. I will not have my daughter's life put at risk over something that can easily be solved with a letter to the dean and a temporary hiatus from your coursework."

The word *daughter* hangs in the air between us, heavier than fog. I drop my eyes to the gleaming surface of his desk and do my damndest to ignore it.

"I don't want to take a hiatus," I whisper.

"Then we will enroll you in online classes."

"And my internship?" I ask, lifting my eyes again. "How can I see patients, or practice therapy, or learn to diagnose from behind a computer screen?"

His head shakes. "The palace has many resources. Connections at every academic institution in the world. Should you decide to abdicate at the end of our trial, I will personally ensure you are settled in whichever field you choose to pursue."

"But—"

"Emilia. On this point, I will not bend. I cannot."

My hands curl into fists. I glare at the man across the desk — at the unyielding set to his shoulders and the firm press of his mouth — and suddenly realize where my stubborn streak comes from.

Rock, meet hard place.

The last thing I want to do is give up my internship. I worked my ass off to land it. But I'm smart enough to know that without intervention, it's only a matter of time before Linus releases a royal statement about me to the press. And once that tea is spilled... there'll be no getting it back in the cup. I'll be stuck forever in this life.

The heir apparent.

The crown princess.

As far as I can see... this negotiation is the only sliver of a chance I've got at hanging onto my dreams. My life. My identity. My home.

"There must be something else," Linus interjects suddenly, seeming to read my thoughts. "Something of equal or greater value to you, that I can offer in exchange."

My eyes hold his for a long moment. "There is one thing."

"Name it."

"My house... *Nina's* house."

He stills at the mention of Mom. "What about it?"

"The mortgage..." I suck in a sharp breath. "With the internship on top of my classes, I had to cut back on my waitressing hours. It's been tough to keep up with the payments."

"Ah. And what is the outstanding balance?"

I pause. "Around a hundred-thousand dollars."

"I see."

"It wasn't Mom's fault. The house was nearly paid off. But when she died..." I look up into his eyes, shame swallowing me whole. "Between the hospital bills and my school expenses, I had no choice but to consolidate our debt. A second mortgage was the only option I could think of to make ends meet."

"I understand." He considers me gravely. "I assume you would like me to absorb that balance, as part of our agreement."

The only thing I hate more than asking for help is asking for money. It makes me feel *dirty* somehow. Brimming with mortification and wounded pride that I can't handle things on my own. But that feeling doesn't compare with the devastation I experience whenever I think about losing the house.

Every room, every wall, every floorboard is embedded with memories of my mother. Cooking elaborate meals together in the tiny kitchen, reading by the old wood stove in the back room, watching black and white movies beneath a blanket on chilly autumn nights. I can't bear the thought of losing my last remaining link to her.

"Yes," I whisper, my voice cracking. "If you help with the house, I'll do whatever you want."

"Then consider it done," Linus agrees easily, as though I've asked to borrow a fiver for a carton of milk, not a payment-in-full on my mortgage. "I'll have a check sent to the bank tomorrow."

Relief floods through me. Maybe tonight, for the first time in months, I'll be able to fall asleep without tossing and turning, dreaming of envelopes marked PAST DUE in red ink, worrying about the dire financial hole I've dug myself into.

"Thank you," I murmur.

"Is there anything else you want?"

I shake my head, at a loss for words.

"Then terms are as follows: I will assume financial responsibility for your house, arrange for some of your personal belongings to be delivered here — along with Mr. Harding, if he so chooses — and assist you in finding a new internship, in the event of abdication. In return, you will live here — and, when it's safe, at the palace — until my coronation in one month. You will be fully at my disposal for formal events, public appearances... whatever I see fit. You will take twice daily *princess lessons*, as you so charmingly christened them. And, above all, you will keep an open mind about the role you would play, should you choose to accept your position as my heir." He pins me with a grave stare. "Are we are in agreement?"

"Yes," I say, exhausted by the mere prospect of the weeks that lie ahead of me. "We are in agreement."

"Shall we shake on it?" He extends a hand across his desk. "To make it official?"

Slowly, I reach out and slide my palm into his sturdy grip. He doesn't pump my hand up and down in a normal shake — he simply holds it, squeezing lightly as he stares into my eyes. It's a strangely poignant moment, all things considered. As is the realization that, if Linus weren't my biological father...

I think I'd probably like him.

"Thank you, again," I say haltingly, pulling back. I tuck my hands beneath my thighs. "For not laughing at me. For hearing me out. For... *negotiating*."

He nods, somber as ever. "I'm rather impressed, actually. Only a very poor leader would accept a deal blindly, without questioning the terms and assuring their own interests."

Did my father just... compliment me?

I don't know what to say, so I simply nod.

"Next time, don't fold your hand so fast," he adds in a lighter tone. "If you'd held your ground, you might've talked me down on the princess lessons."

My mouth falls open. "But— you said those terms were non-negotiable!"

"Consider this your first lesson: everything is negotiable, Emilia. The letter of law, the will of the people... even the word of a king."

"Not fair," I grumble. "I want a re-do."

"Second lesson: there are no quote-unquote *re-do*s in politicking."

I sigh. "Well, that sucks."

"And so the trial begins." His mouth turns up at one corner. "Tomorrow, at your first tutoring sessions, I'll be sure to have your instructor teach you all the best methods to *flirt and finger-wave* like a — what was it you said?"

"Tiara-wearing airhead," I murmur.

He chuckles — the first time I've ever heard him laugh. It's a rusty sound, as though he doesn't do it very often. "By god, you are so very much like your mother."

I look up sharply. "You think?"

"I do." The laugher bleeds out of his tone, replaced by a heart-rending sadness. "She was willful. Beautiful. A true force to be reckoned with."

"She was." My eyes are stinging precariously. I push to my feet and turn for the door. "I really should be going, now."

"Emilia." His voice halts me halfway to the exit.

I glance back.

"I am so very sorry you lost her. I should've said that before." His eyes press closed. "I'm sure you miss her with each breath."

Why does he sound like he's speaking from experience?

Before I can do something foolish, like ask the question aloud, I slip out of his study and close the door firmly behind me.

CHAPTER NINE

I PULL OPEN A CABINET, grimace, and slam it back closed.

"Miss Emilia," the timid housekeeper, Patricia, whispers for the third time in as many minutes. "If you'd just tell me what you need, I'll be happy to make it for you…"

"I told you already," I mutter, yanking open another cabinet. *Pots and pans.* I promptly shut it and move on. "The only thing I *need* is something to keep me occupied. I'm going insane in this empty house, just sitting around doing nothing all day."

"Yes, miss."

Another cabinet, this one full of cleaning products.

The next, brimming with brightly polished candlesticks.

Moving on.

Much like the rest of the manor, the kitchen is massive. It took me nearly thirty minutes of wandering down empty corridors to even locate it, tucked away in the basement, accessible only by a narrow servant's stairwell. I descended, expecting a dark, dank, windowless room without air circulation. Instead, I found a lovely space with narrow skylights by the ceiling that allow in soft shafts of late-afternoon light.

Much to the confusion of household staff — who assured me they could make me anything I desired, if only I'd allow them — I spent the first twenty minutes simply walking around in awe, skimming my fingers along the set of gleaming copper pots that hang from an overhead rack, examining the brick oven where three fresh breads are baking, marveling at the dum-waiters embedded in the walls, used to quickly run dishes up and down during dinner parties.

Between the stainless steel counter tops, three modern glass-front refrigerators, and more cooking implements than I've ever seen in one place… it's rather different from the kitchen I grew up using — a narrow galley with barely any room to move around and a gas range so old, the burners don't light without a match.

But I bet no one's ever had as much fun in here as Mom and I did chopping onions on those cracked linoleum counter tops, laughing till the tears were gone.

After my meeting with Linus, I went straight back to my bedroom and stared at the wall for about an hour, wondering if I'd made a massive mistake. Torturing myself, replaying all the counter-arguments I should've used, analyzing all the points I forgot to touch on during our negotiation, until I thought my head might explode from the strain of it all.

I needed a distraction. Something to take my mind off the future. Preferably, something involving semi-sweet chocolate morsels and a nice rush of sugar. I needed…

Cookies.

So, I put aside my worries about bumping into Carter or Chloe or — *god forbid* — their mother, and set out to find the kitchen. Now, if I could only find the flour, I'd be in business…

"Dammit," I mutter, opening another cabinet. This one is full of what appears to be an antique china set.

"Miss, are you sure I can't assist with—"

"I'm sure!" I cut her off, shaking my head in exasperation and muttering to myself. "Seriously, how do rich people live like this? What do they *do* with all this free time?" I pull open another cabinet. *Spices.* I'm getting closer. "No chores to complete? No meals to prepare? Food appears magically on the table, dirty clothes vanish without me lifting a finger… I feel like I'm living with freaking house elves."

"I apologize, miss," Patricia says, sounding near tears.

"Oh, please don't be upset!" I whirl to face her, guilt flooding me. "I know you're just doing your job. It's *me*. I'm not used to sitting around all day without pulling my weight. I go a bit stir-crazy without anything to keep me occupied. Can you understand that?"

"Of course, miss."

I smile, but she doesn't return it — she's too busy chewing her bottom lip. Clearly, she's not used to royal guests making themselves at home in her domain.

With a sigh, I resume my search for ingredients. I've nearly given up hope when I pull open the final set of white doors and find a narrow inset pantry, fully stocked with baking supplies.

"Of course, it's the last one I open…"

I laugh as I grab the containers marked FLOUR and SUGER off the shelf, cradle them to my chest, and carry them over to a nearby prep table. The Lockwood Estate's heavy stand mixer is far nicer quality than the one I have back home, but it doesn't look much different in terms of basic mechanics. I'm sure I can figure out how to use it easily enough.

Patricia wrings her hands in silent agony as she watches me make trips back and forth from the pantry, lining up my items in a neat row — baking soda, salt, vanilla extract, chocolate chips.

When she sees me heading for her immaculately organized refrigerator, she can't quite contain her sound of distress.

"Miss, are you *quite* sure you wouldn't prefer me to do that for you? If you'll only dictate the recipe—"

"Sorry," I say wryly, plucking two eggs from a carton. "I'm that crazy person who actually enjoys making things for herself."

"Crazy person?" A warm, familiar voice cuts through the room. "*That*, I will vouch for."

I'm so startled, I drop both eggs to the floor. I hear the unmistakable crunch of shells on tile along with a shriek from the housekeeper as she watches yolk spreading across her floor, but I don't care. I'm already in motion — flying across the kitchen into Owen's waiting arms.

"You're here!" I cry as he crushes me to his chest, breathing him in. He smells so good. Safe. Solid. Secure.

Like home.

"Of course I'm here. You think I'd let them lock you up and throw away the key without putting up a fight? Not a chance, Ems."

"My hero," I tease in a swooning voice.

He laughs. "Yeah, well, it wasn't exactly easy. I probably called a hundred times, screaming as an apathetic operator fed me the same bullshit line about *confidential royal protocol* and *routine security procedure*. I was scared out of my fucking head that something had happened to you."

"God." I squeeze him tighter. "I'm really sorry."

"Not your fault. It's the bastards who dragged you here," he mutters darkly.

"Owen, the thing is—"

"You know, I'm not actually sure why they changed their minds. I guess I must've worn them down, though, because about an hour ago this fancy black town car pulls up outside my apartment and the driver tells me to get in. *By order of the king.* How insane is that? I felt like I was in an action movie." He snorts. "Not a good one."

A flash of guilt moves through me. I know *exactly* why he's suddenly here with me — it has nothing to do with his extensive cellphone charges and everything to do with the deal I made in Linus' study two hours ago. I don't have the heart to correct him.

"Thank you for coming," I whisper, blinking away tears. "I really can't believe you're here."

"Me? What about *you?*" he counters, pulling back to look down at me. There's an undeniable fissure of concern between his narrowed brown eyes. "Seriously, Ems... what the fuck are you still doing here?" His gaze darts around the kitchen, zeroing in on the ingredients behind me. "Besides, apparently, baking cookies for the goddamn enemy."

Flinching, I drop my arms to my sides.

"I mean it, Ems. What the hell is going on? I charge in, expecting to find you locked up in some bedroom like a prisoner of war, fighting tooth and nail for your freedom... Imagine my surprise to see you're perfectly content being kidnapped."

"That's not true!"

"Isn't it?"

"Owen, *stop.* You don't know what you're talking about!"

"Then explain it to me.

I run both hands through my hair. "It's complicated."

"What's so complicated about it?" he asks. "Grab your shit and let's get the hell out of here. Away from these people. Back to our life."

My eyes widen a shade. "I... Owen, I can't."

"What the hell do you mean, you can't?"

I dart a glance behind me at Patricia, who's down on her hands and knees cleaning the egg yolks off the floor, in plain earshot of every word we're saying. If I thought there was any chance at all she'd allow it, I'd get down there and help her... but I'm wise enough not to try.

"Come with me, okay?" I plead with my best friend, grabbing his limp hand and threading our fingers together. "I'll explain. Just... not here."

He stares at me stoically for a moment before returning my hand-squeeze. Calling an apology over my shoulder to Patricia, I lead him out of the kitchen and up the stairs. Foreboding fills the pit of my stomach, weighing me down a bit more with each step we ascend.

Why do I have a feeling I'm about to make an even bigger mess than the one I just left behind on the immaculate kitchen floors?

♛

IT'S A GORGEOUS AUTUMN DAY.

The snow-capped mountains behind the manor make a picture-perfect backdrop for our walk through the gardens. Two guards trail us at a respectful distance — mute shadows, ever watchful as we wind a path around topiaries and bubbling fountains. The maze of carefully tended plots is beautiful despite the lack of summer blooms. On any other day, we'd be enjoying the view, laughing and joking about trivial things, sharing stories and making plans for the future.

Today, we are a chasm of deep silence.

He hasn't said a word since I told him about the deal I made with Linus. I can't say I blame him. When he arrived earlier, he thought he was here to rescue me. My real life knight-in-shining-armor. Instead, he learned the princess didn't need any saving. In fact, she'd already struck a deal with the wicked king.

I shiver as the breeze picks up. My light cotton blouse and thin navy pants may be fashionable in the eyes of the palace personal shoppers, but they're not exactly suited to spending time outdoors in the brisk Germanian climate. I can't help thinking their decision not to include a coat in my new wardrobe was an intentional move to keep me from straying too far from the manor.

Nice try, assholes.

I've begun rubbing my hands together for warmth when Owen stops walking, shrugs out of his sturdy olive green jacket, and passes it to me.

"Here. Take it."

My throat clogs up. He's always taking care of me — even when he's pissed.

"Thanks," I murmur, pulling it on. Made of heavy canvas-like material, it's practically the length of a dress on my petite frame, the sleeves hanging down far past my hands. He can't quite hide the twitching of his lips when he sees how ridiculous I look wearing it.

"Owen—"

His lips flatten into a frown again. "Don't."

"You don't even know what I was going to say."

"Of course I do. I've known you your whole damn life." He sighs deeply. "You're going to try to justify why this is the right decision for you, in the long run. Because you've no doubt already made a list of pros and cons, and rehearsed all your little talking points in your bathroom mirror…"

My cheeks flame. He really *does* know me.

"But I'm not interested in any of that fake bullshit, Emilia. I'm your best friend. I want the truth."

"I told you the truth! I'd never lie to you, you know that."

"Don't try to pass off your *trial period* as an elaborate plan to abdicate the throne." He shakes his head. "If that were the case, you'd walk out those front gates with me right now and never look back."

"Owen, it's not that simple…"

89

"It *is* that simple." His eyes are undeniably sad. "But we both know you won't. Because there's a part of you that *wants* to be here. A part of you that needs to know what it would be like to wear that crown."

I lock my jaw, not contradicting him. I can't.

We don't lie to each other.

"You can tell yourself you're only doing this so he'll pay your mortgage, so you can keep the house you grew up in and still maintain your anonymity... but I know there's a part of you that's curious what it would be like, living in places like this instead." He jerks his thumb back toward the Lockwood Estate. "Servants at your beck and call. A bonafide princess, right out of a fairy tale."

"And what if I *am* curious?" I snap defensively, growing tired of his judgmental tone. "Is that such a crime?"

"It is if it means selling your soul to these people!"

"*These people?* You mean my *biological father?*"

"Yeah, the one who never wanted shit to do with you until yesterday? I recall him pretty well," he mutters. "Really pathetic to see you fold like a fucking lawn chair the first second he gives you any attention at all."

Tears spring to my eyes. "Not all of us were raised in a family like yours, Owen. Perfect parents, perfect house, perfect sisters. Some of us have some unresolved issues that, *gee*, it might be nice to deal with when finally given the chance. I thought, of all people, you would understand that. Maybe I was wrong."

"You think I don't know you have baggage? I've been the one hauling it around for you for *twenty fucking years!*" he roars at the top of his lungs, so loud I'm surprised it doesn't bring the guards running.

"Owen—" My voice cracks as a tear races down my cheek. I honestly can't believe he just said that to me. Or, more accurately, *screamed* that at me. In all our years of friendship, he's never acted this way. I can't help wondering if this reaction is about more than just me, getting to know my father.

His furious expression crumbles a bit when he sees the tears.

"I'm sorry," he grits out after a moment, his anger tightly in check. "I didn't mean to yell, Ems."

I nod stiffly.

"I just…" He takes a step closer to me. "I can't stand by and watch as you're manipulated into a life you never wanted."

I'm silent.

"I don't want you getting swallowed up by these people."

"I won't. Give me a little credit, Owen."

He takes a step forward, until our faces are a half-foot apart, and leans down to take my face between his hands. His thumb brushes away a teardrop. "I'm worried I'm going to lose you."

"You could never lose me, Owen." I reach up and place my hand on top of his. "Even if I stay, even if I don't abdicate… nothing will change. Not when it comes to you and me."

Something flashes in his eyes. He opens his mouth to say something, but he never gets the chance, because we're suddenly not alone. Two people in tight athletic clothes jog around the bend in the path, practically barreling straight into us. We spring apart instantly.

"Well, isn't *this* cozy," Chloe drawls, taking in the sight of us with laser-sharp interest. Her red ponytail swings jauntily as a grin spreads across her face.

I know what this must look like to them — me, wearing Owen's jacket, gazing upward as he cups my face. Not two friends coming to terms with some big changes, but a couple, sharing a stolen moment in a secret garden.

Why do you care what they think? I ask myself, even as my eyes cut straight to Carter. My heart starts to thud. I haven't seen him since last night — haven't spoken to him since our screaming match in the hallway. There's a certain twisted irony in the fact that the last words I hissed at him were an adamant declaration that I don't have a boyfriend. His cold cerulean eyes meet mine, utterly devoid of all emotion, and somehow I know he's thinking the exact same thing.

I swallow hard.

"Who's the regulation hottie?" Chloe asks, planting her hands on her hips. "And where do I get myself one?"

"This is Owen," I tell her, not offering any more detail than absolutely necessary. "Owen, these are Linus' step-children. Chloe and—" *Why is it so hard to say his name when he's looking at me like that?* "And Carter."

Carter's eyes break with mine and slide to Owen's, his severe expression intensifying. I feel Owen stiffen at my side, rising to his full height as he returns the look. Neither man says anything — not out loud, anyway. But whatever silent communication they're having isn't a good one, judging by the frigid silence that spreads over our small group.

"It's nice to meet you," Chloe interjects with forced brightness, her eyes sharp as they flit back and forth between her brother and my best friend. "If all of Emilia's friends are this hot, I think maybe this *unwanted-little-sister* thing won't be so bad."

I force a thin laugh.

Owen glances at her cooly. "Emilia is not your sister."

"*Owen,*" I mutter. "She was only kidding. Don't be an ass."

It's clear he's not in a joking mood, though, as his eyes return to mine. "I don't give a shit if she was kidding or not. Do you even know anything about these new *siblings* you've decided to live with? Probably not, since you avoid royal gossip like the plague."

"For good reason," I insist.

"Not when you expect me to leave you here alone with them!"

"Emilia's a big girl," Chloe says, amused. "She can make up her own mind about us."

"I think that's what he's afraid of," Carter adds lowly.

Owen tenses. "Don't you speak to me about Emilia. *Ever.*"

"Why?" Carter smirks. "Afraid you'll hear something you don't like?"

"Now, now, boys," Chloe murmurs. "Play nice or we'll kick you out of the sandbox."

Owen ignores her, turning back to me. His eyes are full of such sharp desperation, it scares me. "Don't you understand? These people represent *everything* that's wrong with this monarchy. They reap all the benefits of royalty without any of the responsibility. They're just... *leeches,* sucking the lifeblood from our taxpayers."

Chloe snorts.

He glances at her. "What, you disagree? You've made so many visits to rehab, I'm pretty sure your next OD is free." His eyes flicker to Carter. "And your brother has bedded half the damn country!"

The warning growl that rattles in Carter's throat is scary enough to send a chill down my spine.

"That's *enough,* Owen!" I hiss, totally mortified. "I don't even recognize you right now!"

"Right back at you," he snaps. "God, Ems, I know you're looking for a family, but I think you deserve better than a coke head and a walking STD."

Carter takes a threatening stride forward, hands fisted at his sides. "Care to say that again, pretty boy?"

Owen turns to him and the dark expression on his face is like nothing I've ever seen. "You don't scare me, little lordling."

"Then you're either very brave or very stupid." Cerulean eyes glitter. "I'm guessing I know which one."

"Seeing as I'm not the husband of a desperate housewife

eager for an affair with some half-royal prick… I think I'm safe from you." Owen leans in, voice dropping. "Isn't that your usual MO — bang the wife, humiliate the husband, ruin the marriage? See, unlike Emilia, I *do* read the papers."

Chloe sucks in a sharp breath.

Carter's face goes totally dark — clearly, Owen has struck a nerve. When he steps toward us, I feel my pulse stutter inside my chest.

"You know, you seem a bit preoccupied with my sexual conquests." Carter smiles without even the slightest trace of humor. "Don't worry. There are no women in my bedroom here — which, as it happens, is right across the hall from Emilia's." He pauses meaningfully. "I'll be sure to keep a *close* eye on her for you, mate."

Owen actually flinches. "If you so much as touch a hair on her head…"

"Oh, I won't," Carter goads. "Not unless she asks me to, of course."

"Please, stop," I beg, voice cracking under the strain. "Both of you! This is absurd."

I grab Owen's arm, trying to shake some sense into him, but he's beyond my reach — lost in a dark, consuming fury. Staring at his face, at those deep brown eyes, that floppy blond hair I've always loved so much… for the first time in my life, I feel like I'm looking at a stranger.

When Carter advances another step, Chloe throws out an arm to halt him. I do the same with Owen, pressing him back with all the strength I possess. I can feel his chest rising and falling rapidly, even through the thick sleeve of the jacket. Both men look like they're one word away from beating each other senseless on the idyllic garden path. There's so much testosterone in the air, I'm surprised a five o'clock shadow doesn't break out on my jaw, just from breathing it in.

Chloe's wild eyes meet mine. "Maybe you two should go."

I couldn't agree more.

With a grimace, I step fully in front of Owen and start pushing him backward, trying to force him out of the line of fire. He resists, legs locked firmly in place.

"Let's go, Harding," I snap, shoving his chest. "Don't make me call your mother. You know I will. And we both know Belinda will be *pissed*."

His eyes flicker to mine and for just a second, I see a trace of the boy I used to know beneath this posturing, unrecognizable alpha male.

"Please," I whisper.

With a sigh, he clenches his jaw, spins, and starts walking down the path — head bowed, hands fisted, shoulders tense beneath the fabric of his long-sleeve shirt. I cast a quick glance back at Chloe and Carter before I follow, totally at a loss for words. I'm stunned by Owen's behavior. Totally mortified by the things he said about them.

"Oh, don't you dare apologize," Chloe cuts me off before I can, her lips twisting up in a small smile. "Things are finally getting interesting around here."

With a grateful nod in her direction, I turn and dart after Owen. I never spare so much as a glance at Carter. But the whole way down the path, I feel the weight of those too-blue eyes burning into my back like a fire I cannot extinguish, no matter how hard I try.

CHAPTER TEN

AFTER THE OWEN INCIDENT, I thought life at The Lockwood Estate couldn't possibly get worse.

I was so very wrong.

"Remember: chin up, shoulders back, grip *delicate*." Lady Morrell stares down her long, hooked nose with disapproval. "It is a spoon, not a hand grenade. Your index finger should rest on the silver, light as a a winged hummingbird taking pollen from a flower."

She's full of these flowery, over-the-top analogies. Already today I've been instructed on how to glide around a dance floor *like a soaring hawk taking flight over a pink dawn sky* and curtsy low to the floor *like a setting sun sinking slowly toward the ever-fixed horizon*.

Whenever I start to question why I'm subjecting myself to this, I focus on the hundred thousand dollar light at the end of the tunnel. That's usually enough to keep me from bolting.

"Very well, Lady Morrell." I adjust my grip for the tenth time. "How's this?"

"Wrong. Utterly wrong! Here, let me demonstrate again…"

I swallow a scream. I'm not sure how much more of this I can take before I give up and race back to my rooms…

Like a swift cheetah crossing the Serengeti!

I snort in an unladylike fashion that earns me a glare from my tutor.

As predicted, princess lessons have been completely insufferable. Six hours a day — three in the morning, three more in the afternoon — of Lady Morrell lecturing on the merits of proper decorum, table manners, royal address, and Germanian customs. By Wednesday, my head is so full of banal information, I've reached a saturation point.

Use 'Your Majesty' to address a king or queen. 'Your Highness' for a prince or princess. 'Your Grace' for a duke or duchess. 'My Lord' for barons, earls, and knights.

Do not curtsey to anyone of lower rank.

Never cross your legs; always cross your ankles.

Elbow-length gloves are to be worn for all official ceremonies of state.

Manicures shall be allowed in nude or pastel shades only.

No autographs or signatures of any kind.

No unauthorized photographs.

No public displays of affection.

No use of social media platforms.

No.

No.

No.

The word has been thrown around so often, I've begun to wonder if there's anything a princess actually *is* authorized to do — besides smile and wave during scheduled appearances at boring social functions.

Lady Morrell insists she's only trying to prepare me for what she calls my *first royal test* — which, as she frequently reminds me, is approaching at the speed of light. I can't say I'm thrilled by the prospect of attending the funeral on Sunday with the Lancasters

— even flying under the radar, posing as just another aide in their entourage. The mere thought of it sends butterflies bursting into flight in the pit of my stomach.

So many things could go wrong.

I'm not remotely prepared to appear in front of anyone as *royalty* yet. That much has been made glaringly obvious by Morrell's ever-exasperated expression when she glances my way, whether I'm stumbling through dance lessons, fumbling royal titles, or using the incorrect cutlery during dinner courses.

I try to avoid looking at the towering grandfather clock on the other side of the dining room, knowing it's only going to disappoint me, but I can't help myself. *Four o'clock.* Still another full hour before I'm free. I readjust my grip on the spoon and attempt to take a sip of my soup without, and I quote, *slurping like a teenage boy drinking a cola at the cinema.*

I suppose the only blessing to Morrell's maddening tutelage is that it's keeping me too busy to think much about Owen… or to bump into Chloe and Carter in the hallways of our shared penitentiary. After five days cooped up in this place, I'm sure they're both chafing to escape just as much as I am. But the King's Guard still hasn't lifted the security lockdown. It's unlikely they will before the funeral, now that the fire has officially been classified as foul play by the arson investigators.

I spent last night locked in my bedroom, scrolling through news updates on my battered old laptop — which was finally returned to my possession along with my school textbooks, cellphone, and a duffle of clothing selected from my dresser at home. I try not to think too hard about one of the solemn, suit-wearing guards digging through my underwear drawer and touching all my things.

Because…

Ew.

I scrolled through article after article, reading headlines and theories from journalists all over the world about potential motives, likely suspects, possible political implications. The outpouring of grief was immeasurable, bringing the whole world to its knees. And the news that it was murder, rather than tragedy, that took the lives of our king and queen was a kick to the stomach while we were already down on the ground.

Someone did this. Killed the king and queen, along with five members of their staff. Put the crown prince in a coma from which he may never wake. And that someone is still at large.

It's hard to conceive how something like this could happen. Harder still to imagine that there are no witnesses, no leads...

Nothing.

The investigation hasn't yielded anything concrete — at least, not according to Simms, who I bumped into on my way back to my room after my lessons, yesterday. As for the rest of the household, everyone seems content to avoid each other. I haven't seen Octavia since the night I arrived, nor have I encountered Linus since our meeting the other day.

Occasionally, I'll hear Carter or Chloe walking the halls of the wing where all our rooms are located, but I have no idea how they spend the majority of their days. After the incident in the garden, neither of them has tried to make conversation. Frankly, I don't blame them.

I wouldn't want to talk to me, either.

My eyes press closed with horror, thinking back on it... as well as the massive fight I had with Owen, afterward.

Fight. With. Owen.

I'm fighting with Owen.

No matter how many times I say it, the concept is difficult to wrap my mind around. Before this, there's never been a point in my life when we weren't speaking. Sure, we've had minor spats over the years... but nothing to this degree. I don't think I'll ever forget the look on his face when I walked him to the front gates, the other night, and asked him to leave.

I just need a little time, I told him, avoiding his gaze. *I'll call you when I'm ready to talk.*

The truth is, though, I need a hell of a lot more than time. I need to figure out if I'll ever be able to look him in the eyes again without recalling the stinging lash of his words. Not just the awful ones he directed at Chloe and Carter... the ones he said to me.

Pathetic.

Naive.

Broken.

I've always thought there were no lines between us left to cross, no boundaries remaining to push. I see now how foolish that was. The people who love us most are the best equipped to destroy us. After all, we've spent years handing over the ammunition, piece by piece, giving them everything they'll ever need to inflict maximum damage.

The most twisted part of it is that, angry as I am, I still find myself wanting to call him, just to hear the comforting rasp of his voice. Twice today I've caught myself reaching for my cellphone — which, as it happens, was mysteriously scrubbed of all social media applications before being returned to my possession. I managed to stop myself before the call connected, but I know it's only a matter of time before I cave in to the urge.

Owen has always been the person I turn to when I'm hurt; I'm not sure how to cope, now that he's the one doing the hurting.

Lady Morrell clears her throat, bringing my focus back to the present.

"I think you have finally mastered the soup course," she informs me, nodding her approval. "Perhaps you are ready to graduate to something more complex."

"Foreign affairs?" I ask hopefully.

"Not quite." Her lips twitch as she swaps out my bowl for a small plate. "*Salads.*"

"Joy of joys," I mutter, resisting the urge to bang my head against the tabletop until I knock myself unconscious.

One more hour.

One hundred thousand dollars.

I pick up the damn salad fork.

LATER THAT NIGHT, I'm lying in bed attempting to get through one of the dense books Linus sent up for me — a heavy, leather-bound tome called *Germania: Honor Throughout History* — when someone knocks on my door.

"Come in," I call lazily, expecting it's one of the housekeepers, here to stoke the fire or fluff my pillows or deliver yet another plate of warm chocolate-chip cookies — as they have every night since my failed baking endeavor. At first, I thought it was a nice gesture, but now I'm pretty sure it's just Patricia's insurance policy, keeping me out of her kitchen by any means necessary.

The door swings inward on soundless hinges. I glance up from the pages and nearly have a heart attack when I see the woman standing there, her perfectly coiffed auburn hair offset by teardrop earrings, an elegant gray dress, and sensible heels.

"Octavia!" I sit up so abruptly, the book tumbles from my grasp. It hits the floor with a dull thud. "Wh— what are you doing here?"

Her eyes narrow as they take me in. Lavender hair in a messy bun on top of my head, makeup smudged beneath my eyes, dressed in a loose t-shirt and a pair of buttery soft yoga pants. I scramble off the bed, nervously tucking a tendril of hair behind one ear. It takes all my resolve not to flinch as she sidles closer, heels clicking ominously against the hardwood floor.

"I see you are..." She sniffs delicately. "Settling in."

"Yes, Octavia. I mean ma'am. *Madame*. Err... *Highness?*" I fumble horribly. Lady Morrell would be devastated to learn all her careful lessons have gone to utter waste.

"I have not yet been given a royal title." Octavia's expression is totally devoid of warmth. "When I am officially named queen consort after Linus' coronation next month, you can refer to me as Your Majesty. Until then..." Her eyes narrow to pinpricks. "Frankly, I'm not sure you'll need to address me at all, but if you cannot avoid doing so during a social engagement, you may call me Lady Lancaster."

God, she's so cold. I don't know what I did to get on her bad side so quickly — besides, you know, *exist* — but I find myself shivering despite the warmth from the fire.

She looks around at my belongings, scattered over every surface. The half-eaten plate of cookies, the shirt I wore earlier crumpled on the armchair, a hefty pile of Linus' books on my side table. She traces her finger across the embossed cover of the volume at the top of the stack, a flicker of disgust moving across her face as she digests the title.

Kings and Queens: The Lancaster Legacy

"I assume there's a reason for this unexpected visit," I say, voice dripping with false sweetness.

"Certainly." She turns back toward me, folding her arms across her chest. "Linus has informed me that you'll be attending the funeral alongside our family."

I think she'd sound more pleased by the prospect of an impending colonoscopy.

"The seamstresses will be coming tomorrow at noon with a selection of dresses for Chloe and myself. I've been... *advised*... I must extend that invitation to you as well." She scans me up and down. "Seeing as you cannot be trusted to dress yourself, we will have something proper selected for you."

I reel back, but manage to force a smile onto my face. "How very kind. I'll be sure to pick something…" I pause meaningfully, just to annoy her. "*Fit for a queen.*"

Her shoulders stiffen with barely-contained outrage. "Wonderful."

"Well, if that's all…" I look pointedly toward the door. My message could not be more clear.

Get the hell out of my room.

"Not quite." Her lips purse in a thin-lipped smile that scares me far more than any of her frowns. "There is one more matter I need to discuss with you."

My brows lift, waiting.

"You had a friend visit the premises, several days ago. Owen Harding. Is that correct?"

I go still. "Yes."

"Mr. Harding did pass the initial security clearance checks, which allowed him access to this estate. Thankfully, I *personally* insisted the King's Guard dig a bit deeper into his past." She takes a step closer, eyes never shifting from mine. "We can't be too careful when it comes to your safety, now can we?"

My heart is pounding double-speed inside my chest. "Your concern for me is truly heartwarming, Octavia. But I assure you — *unnecessary.*"

Her smile widens. "Unfortunately, I must disagree. The secondary search uncovered some… shall we say… *problematic* connections in Mr. Harding's past." She shakes her head, feigning distress. "It seems he has ties to several anti-monarchist groups. Perhaps even a radical cell of anarchists, determined to overthrow the crown at any cost."

My mouth falls open. "*What*?!"

"It's certainly a relief we caught wind of it now, before things…" She pauses. "Escalated."

I'm not sure whether to laugh or cry at the utter absurdity of the words coming out of her mouth. "You must be joking."

"Safety is not a joking matter, or one we take lightly. Especially in the current climate." She sighs, as though she's terribly troubled. "Never fear — only a few more pieces of evidence, and we should have enough to take him off the streets. For good."

I freeze. "*No.*"

"Oh, yes. It's merely a matter of whether we *choose* to keep looking. Do you understand me, Emilia?"

Oh, I understand you perfectly, you heartless hag.

"Octavia, please..." My voice breaks. My heart slams against my ribs, a mad tattoo. "Owen isn't a part of any terrorist cell! He's not an anti-monarchist. Sure, he may've participated in a few nonviolent protests, a political march or two on the university campus... but he's never done anything remotely illegal, let alone *radical.*"

"Nevertheless," she murmurs smugly, victorious. "You are not to contact him again, either in person or otherwise. I've ensured that he's already been blacklisted from all royal properties and functions. And don't worry, dear — if he attempts to trespass on *any* Lancaster land — Lockwood Estate included — I will personally see to it that he is jailed for conspiracy against the crown." She leans forward, her voice intent. "You see... I will do *whatever* is necessary to protect the members of my family. I hope this proves that to you."

"You can't do this," I whisper, hate blazing from my eyes. "You *can't.*"

"It's already done."

"I'll talk to Linus!" I snap, stepping forward. "I'll get him to reverse the order."

She laughs — actually throws her head back and laughs at me, like I'm a puppet and she's the one holding all my strings, making me dance. "You foolish little girl. Did you honestly think, because you caught his ear for a single afternoon, that he cares about you? That, because he sent you a few books and needs a new heir, he's going to suddenly step in and become a father figure? *You're wrong.* The only person Linus Lancaster serves is Linus Lancaster. You will find out for yourself just how little you matter to him, as soon as your interests stop aligning with his own."

"You're wrong," I seethe quietly.

"Am I?" She steps closer. "It may be called the King's Guard, but everyone in this household answers to one person — *me.* Not Linus, locked away in his study with his manuscripts and his memos and his quaint meetings over tea. Certainly not *you.*" She makes a mocking *tsk* noise with her lips. "So go ahead and try to challenge me, girl. I will have Owen Harding locked up in a royal prison cell so fast, it will make your head spin. He'll never see the light of day again, unless *I* see fit to allow it."

"You don't have that kind of power."

"*Try me,*" she dares. "If you're wrong, you'll have only your-self to blame." Her mouth twists. "Alternatively... you can make the smarter choice by yielding to my authority. You can set aside the ridiculous notion that, based on the blood running through your veins, you are somehow entitled to anything but the life you already know, in a very small house with a very small future."

Suddenly, I can see things so clearly. None of this is about Owen. Hell, it's not even about me.

It's about the throne.

It's about *power.*

It's about this shrew of a woman, and the lengths she'll go to take control of the crown.

She wants Germania for herself, I realize, staring at her. *It's not enough to manipulate me, or her children, or her household staff, or her husband... this crazy bitch wants to commandeer the whole damn country.*

Steely resolve fills my bones, fortifying me with new purpose.

I may not know precisely how yet, but I do know one thing: I am going to stop her before she hurts anyone else.

No matter what it takes.

"Octavia," I say in a voice I barely recognize. "I suggest you leave. *Now.*"

She doesn't move. She's enjoying this too much.

"Get out of my room!" I shriek, feeling my control begin to unravel. "You sociopathic, narcissistic monster!"

"Happily." Smiling like we've just traded smalltalk, she turns and starts heading toward the door. "The dress fitting tomorrow. Noon, *sharp*, in the main parlor. Do not be late." She pauses in the threshold to look back at me. "Or, *do*, if you'd like to see what happens when you disobey me. I'd be all too happy to give you a demonstration of my authority." Her head tilts in contemplation. "Owen has two little sisters, doesn't he? Adorable girls. I saw their picture just this afternoon…"

I suck in a sharp breath.

"It would be *such* a shame if anything were to happen to them."

"GET OUT!" I scream at top volume, advancing on her with tears in my eyes. A hate unlike anything I've ever known before boils through my veins. "GET THE HELL OUT OF HERE!"

"Goodnight," she calls serenely, her heels clicking down the hallway like gunshots. "Sweet dreams."

I wait until she's out of sight. Then, with a bellow of rage, I turn and punch my door with every bit of force I possess, unleashing all my anger into the strike — and damn near breaking my hand in the process.

"FUCK!" I wail, crumpling to the floor, clutching my bruised fingers to my chest. I lean against the doorway to my room, tears streaking down my face, breathless with pain and frustration. I'm still reeling from Octavia's threats when I hear the door directly across the hall swing open.

Carter is standing there, dark hair mussed from sleep, looking down at me with concern written all over his face. He must've heard me screaming and come out to investigate. I suck in a breath that has nothing to do with my aching knuckle bones when I see he's barefoot and shirtless, a pair of gray sweatpants riding low on his defined hipbones. My mouth goes dry at the sight of his ab muscles — a perfectly chiseled eight-pack, with a trail of hair leading from his belly button down, down, down....

Sweet Christ.

He starts toward me, making it two steps into the hallway before he catches himself. His expression contorts, flickering through emotions so fast I can't keep track — *pity, concern, desire, anger, worry, disgust* — before settling into an unreadable mask. Taking a step backward, his spine hits the arch of his doorway and, for a moment, I think he's going to disappear back into his bedroom without a word. I'm stunned when, instead, he slides down to the floor so he's sitting across from me, long legs sprawled out in front of him on the hard hallway floor.

He doesn't say anything.

Neither do I.

We just sit there — me, clutching my stupid, damaged hand; him, gazing at me like he can't quite decide whether he wants to crush me to his chest or slam his door in my face. With my good hand, I wipe the tears from my cheeks. There's little point: the instant I try to flex the damaged one, my eyes fill again.

Damn, that hurts.

Carter clears his throat. "You should really put some ice on that."

I glance up sharply and find him carefully studying the angles of my face in the dim hallway light. "I'm fine."

He shrugs indifferently.

"It was stupid," I mutter after a moment. "I know better than to take my anger out on inanimate objects."

"Yeah, well, Octavia has that effect on people." Taking a deep breath that makes his chest muscles contract, he runs a hand through his hair. "As a teenager, I punched so many holes in the walls back in Hightower, they stated calling my chambers the Gypsum Suite." He pauses. "Because the maintenance staff were—"

"Always patching the plaster on your walls," I murmur, a smile tugging up one corner of my mouth. "Clever."

His eyes narrow on my face. "What was the fight about?"

I stare at his bare feet. For some reason, the sight of them is even more mesmerizing than his abs. The Adonis-like Lord Carter Thorne, stripped of his perfectly tailored dress pants and shiny Oxford shoes. A mere mortal, after all.

"Emilia?"

My eyes snap back to his face. I fight the blush staining my cheeks. "Oh, just a regular chat between a girl and her new step-mother, full of thinly-veiled threats, political maneuvering, and outright duplicity. You know, the usual."

He snorts lightly. "Sounds about right."

We fall silent again, just watching each other. It's so quiet in the hallway, I can hear each rhythmic intake of his breath. I stretch my legs out, trying to find a more comfortable position.

"Owen," I say finally.

He goes utterly still.

"She threatened Owen." I swallow hard. "I know you won't be terribly upset to hear it, since you two didn't exactly... get off on the right foot, the other day."

He grunts in agreement.

"But he's my best friend. And now..." I blink back tears. "She's got some pictures of him from an anti-monarchy protest on campus, last fall. She basically implied that... well, that she can make it look a whole lot worse. Like he's a member of a radical fringe group, targeting the crown."

"Can't say I'd be all that surprised if he really was, given the way he talked about me and Chloe."

"It's not true, though!" I cry, anger washing over me anew. "It's just…"

"Octavia attempting to control you."

"Yes. Which I don't understand at all. Even if I ever accept my role — which still remains a big *if* — she'll be the queen. She outranks me."

"For now."

I lift my brows.

He runs a hand through his hair. "You're royal by blood. She's royal by marriage. When she becomes queen, it'll be a symbolic title more than anything. A queen consort is not the same as a queen regnant."

"I'm aware of that."

"Trust me, so is she. She knows the second Linus dies, she'll be out on her ass, to put it bluntly." His blue eyes are intent. "And Linus is not young. Which will just leave…"

"Me," I murmur softly.

"You," he echoes.

As our eyes hold, the air between us starts to feel charged again, that inescapable electrical current running back and forth from him to me. He's a dozen feet away, but I swear I can practically feel his warm touch on my skin.

"We should probably get to bed," I whisper.

Maybe it's my imagination, but I'd swear his eyes flare with heat as he watches my mouth form those words. He quickly smothers the look under a mask of icy indifference. Rising to his feet, he stands in the threshold with his back to me, pausing for the briefest of moments.

"Put some ice on that damn hand."

He's gone a second later, slamming his door with finality. I hear the lock turn over and let a long-held breath rattle from my lungs.

"*Goodnight,*" I whisper to the empty hallway.

The long walk downstairs to the kitchen does absolutely nothing to calm my thundering pulse. And later, when I climb into bed, swollen hand cradled against my chest... I dream of bright blue eyes that somehow always look straight through me, down to the dirty, shattered soul beneath.

CHAPTER ELEVEN

It's 11:55 a.m. and I'm pacing outside the closed parlor doors. I refuse to step into that room until it's absolutely unavoidable.

"She bamboozled you into this too, huh?"

I look up at the sound of Chloe's voice and see her leaning against the wall, watching me ping-pong back and forth. Judging by the warm look on her face, she's not holding a grudge about the Owen incident.

I smile back at her. "Bamboozled is too nice a word for what she did."

"You'll get used to it."

"Is that supposed to make me feel better or worse?"

She laughs, a light tinkling sound. "Neither. But it's the truth. After a while, you'll develop a sort of sixth sense for Octavia's schemes. And once you can anticipate your opponent's moves… it's much easier to evade them."

I shake my head tiredly. "I'm not sure I'm ready for this life."

"No one's ever ready for anything. You just suck it up and do it and hope that eventually the pieces fall into place. Anyone who tells you otherwise is lying."

"That's your best advice? *Suck it up?*"

"Hmm…" She thinks about it for a moment. "Yep."

"Chloe, have you considered a career writing greeting cards? Since you're such a fountain overflowing with heartwarming wisdom?"

"You never know, it could be my true calling. *Watch out, Hall-mark, I'm coming for you!*" Her head tilts. "And, as a side perk, can you imagine the look on Octavia's face if I told her I was getting a job? An actual *job?*"

I gasp. "Like a common peasant?"

"A working schlub!" She throws a hand over her heart. "The outrage!"

"The scandal!'

"The horror of it all!"

"Oh, the humanity!"

We both dissolve into giggles.

"Word of advice? When we're in there, try not to let Octavia rattle you," she says when we've caught our breath. "The more you let your anger show, the happier she'll be. She's like some mythological hell-beast that feeds on misery."

"It would be easier to ignore her if she wasn't threatening people I care about." The clock on the wall begins to chime. I glare at it, as if that might somehow stop time. "Guess that's our cue."

"Don't worry," Chloe whispers conspiratorially, stepping up to my side. "I have something that'll make this experience a lot more enjoyable."

"Cyanide?" I ask, only half-joking.

"Better." She pulls out a small plastic baggie, glances around for Simms or one of the ever-watchful housekeepers, and dumps its contents into her palm. "Take one. Thank me later."

I blink down at the two innocuous-looking gummy bears. "What are they?"

"Just a little something to take the edge off. I call them *Octavia-Tamers*. Makes her at least somewhat bearable to be around — *especially* while doing something this odious."

"Will it really be that bad? Picking out a dress can't possibly take that long, can it? I figured twenty minutes, as a generous estimate."

Chloe snorts. "Oh, you're so new. It might be cute if it weren't so tragic."

"Forty minutes?" I grimace when she shakes her head. "An *hour?*"

"Try two hours of dress selection, followed by another two hours of custom tailoring. Which, if you aren't familiar, generally involves standing in one spot in front of an unflattering mirror while a sadistic seamstress sticks needles into your bodice." Her hand extends again, fingers waggling. "Trust me. You do not want to do this sober."

"I don't know…"

Rolling her eyes, she grabs my palm, presses one bear into it, then promptly tosses the other back into her mouth. "See you on the other side, comrade."

Before I can stop her, she strides for the parlor doors. Frozen with indecision, my eyes flicker back and forth between her hand reaching for the knob and my own, still holding the tiny gummy bear. His tiny face is set in a happy smile. The clock chimes its final toll.

"Sorry, little guy," I murmur. "It's your life or mine."

Two seconds before the door opens, I pop him into my mouth.

I'M NOT GENERALLY what you'd call a *druggie*.

The first time I ever got high, I was fifteen. Owen and I made a makeshift pipe out of an apple core, and we smoked a clump of stale weed he bought from an upperclassman while sitting in the childhood treehouse in his backyard. Probably not our best idea, seeing as I got so dizzy descending the ladder, I fell twelve feet, fractured my arm in two places, and spent the rest of that summer wearing a cast.

Coincidentally, that was also the last *time* I ever got high.

I don't remember much about the experience — mostly just feeling itchy in my own skin, full of restless ideas but devoid of the energy required to put them into practice.

Like I said: I'm not what you'd call a druggie.

But whatever special ingredient Chloe's bears contain is a whole different caliber. I don't feel high at all. In fact, I feel so mellow, I could sink down into the floor and disappear.

Calm. Unflappable. Chill.

The four hours of dress selection and tailoring pass in a hazy blur of zippers and hats and hemlines and lace-covered buttons. Normally, I'd be self-conscious about standing nearly naked in front of a mirror while three strange women measure every square inch of my body... but with the help of Mr. Bear, I feel fully confident in my size six booty and plentiful C-cups — even standing next to Chloe, whose willowy stature could make a super-model insecure enough to skip lunch.

As the afternoon wanes on, Octavia grows increasingly annoyed when her snide comments about my "full figure" fail to inspire a response. She switches tactics, harping on the "atrocious orchid color" of my hair in an attempt to provoke me. The expression on her face as I blithely agree to dye it a more discreet brown before the funeral is truly priceless.

Mr. Bear, today you are my hero.

Followed closely by Chloe.

It's nearly four by the time we're finally released for the day. The effects of the CBD-infused cub are just starting to wear off. Chloe links her arm with mine as we race out of the parlor, a knowing grin splitting her face.

"What's the verdict?"

"Oh captain, my captain! I'll never doubt you again."

"You're welcome." She laughs. "Now, can we *please* go find something to eat? I'm starving."

"I think I have an idea…"

Ten minutes later, we're in the Lockwood home theater, lying on twin leather recliners, staring in awe at the fifteen-foot television. It's set to galaxy mode; a sea of planets and constellations drifting across the screen in a slow parade of shape and color. With the lights dimmed, it's almost like floating out in space amongst the stars.

"Oh my god, these cookies are *so good*," Chloe moans, biting into another. "Where did you say you got them?"

"Patricia. Works in the kitchen. Knows her way around a stand mixer."

"How is it possible that you've been in this family, like, five minutes and the staff already like you more than me? Twenty years living as the Duke of Hightower's stepdaughter, not *once* have I gotten homemade cookies hand-delivered to my suite."

"As if *you* eat cookies on a regular basis?" I snort at the thought.

"Touché."

"Hey, can I ask you something sort of random?"

"Random just so happens to be my favorite kind of question."

"Do you remember your life before Octavia married Linus?"

"Not really. I was only, like, four." She sighs, thinking back. "Carter remembers more than me — probably to his detriment. He was around eight when they got married."

"Why to his detriment?"

"Let's just say there's a reason Carter doesn't believe in marriage or long-term commitment. Growing up in a house with two parents who hate each other doesn't exactly inspire faith in monogamy as a lifestyle choice."

"What was your dad like? Your biological dad."

"Honestly? From what I've pieced together, he was kind of a prick. Gambled away most of his trust fund, was stripped of his familial title, and eventually wrapped his car around a tree driving home drunk from the casino one night — leaving Octavia alone with two young kids to raise on her own and zero prospects to support herself."

"And yet, somehow, she landed a prince."

"I'll say one thing for my mother: she doesn't take no for an answer. Ever. Before she married into the Thorne family, she was nobody. The illegitimate daughter of a stripper who seduced a married lord, thinking she'd get her hands on his fortune. Instead, she got Octavia — who, let's be honest, had to be more of a punishment than a blessing, even as a baby."

"Octavia was illegitimate? No fucking way."

"It's true. Why do you think she loathes you so much?" Chloe's brows lift. "In you, she sees herself."

"Um, *ouch*. Please don't insult me like that."

"No, no, I'm not comparing your personalities. I just mean… you represent everything she's aspired to leave behind. She looks at you and she sees a life she'd rather forget. All the struggle she went through, turning herself from a low-born bastard to a lord's wife to a widow to a duchess… and now, to arguably the most powerful woman in the country."

"Wow."

My mind reels. It's strange to think of Octavia and I having anything in common. Stranger still to think of her at my age — young, vulnerable, desperate. I'd always rather assumed she popped out of the womb wearing that cold, calculating smile of hers.

"Was Linus a good stepfather?" I ask. I'm not even sure where the question comes from but suddenly... there it is, hanging in the air.

Chloe's voice grows thoughtful. "He was, actually — if a little absent. When we were little he traveled a lot, especially after his brother was crowned. King Leopold relied on him greatly as an advisor. I remember long stretches of time without him at Hightower. But when he came back, he'd always have gifts and stories from his trips abroad." The wistful thread in her voice fades. "Of course, Carter and I spent most of our teenage years at different boarding schools in Switzerland, so we didn't see much of Germania except at Christmas and for a few weeks every summer."

"That sounds..."

"Glamorous?"

"I was going to say lonely."

She dunks one end of her cookie into a glass of milk. "Welcome to life as a Lancaster. I think *lonely* is on the royal crest."

"Actually, I'm pretty sure it's a double-headed lion..."

"Shut up."

I grin into the dark. We're quiet for a moment, just watching the stars spin by.

"You know," I murmur. "As crappy as this week has been... I'm happy one good thing came out of it."

"You're talking about the giant-ass tiara they're going to give you at your coronation, right? You could fund a third world country for an entire year, just using the bottom row of diamonds on that thing. Talk about *bling*, baby."

I shoot her a look. "Actually, I was talking about *you*. I've never really had many female friends. It's a nice change of pace."

117

"Ew. Don't get all clingy on me, E. I have commitment issues."

"Deal with it, *C*. And don't for a minute think I missed that line about me being crowned." My eyes roll. "You do realize there's a ninety-nine percent chance I'm going to walk away from all this in a few weeks, right?"

"No." She slams her milk glass onto the table with a bang. "I refuse to accept that. You *cannot* abdicate. If you do… the throne will pass to some distant cousin no one even cares about from the far side of the family tree."

"How far?"

"Far. As in…" She squints, mind churning. "Your grandfather's younger brother's daughter's son."

"Hmm. And how exactly do you know this distant cousin wouldn't make a better leader than me?"

"I don't." She shrugs. "But I can say with at least some degree of confidence that you're not a *complete* idiot. God only knows what kind of moron might come crawling out of the woodwork."

"How sweet."

Her laughter tinkles out in a melodic burst.

A thought occurs to me. "Will the dreaded cousins be there on Sunday? If so, you'll have an opportunity to decide — *with some degree of confidence* — who'd make less of a mess, sitting on the throne."

"Probably." She groans at the prospect. "Everyone and their mother will be there to pay their respects in their finest funeral attire. Should be a positively ghastly affair."

"You make it sound like a bad cocktail party, not a memorial service."

"Funerals aren't for the dead, they're for the living. And, in the case of a royal death, it's more about the spectacle than anything else.

Days of pomp and circumstance, dignitaries flying in from all over the globe… it's a media circus. Frankly, I'd rather remember my aunt and uncle privately, not on display for the sake of the whole world."

"I understand that. When my mom died… I didn't want to share my grief with anyone else. I held it close to my chest for months. I'm not sure why I did it, except that… maybe I thought I'd be giving away a piece of her, somehow, if I talked about her with other people. Does that make any sense?"

Chloe glances over at me. "Maybe it's the gummy bear talking, but yes. It totally does."

I smile and begin to reply, but the sudden buzz of my cellphone on the table between us draws my focus. A quick glance at the screen has my mouth pressing into a flat line. I click the side button to send the call to voicemail.

"Who was it?" Chloe asks, curious.

I hesitate.

"Spill, E."

"It was Owen."

"Ah." She smirks. "And how is the leader of my personal fan club?"

"I don't know. We aren't speaking, at the moment."

And, if your mother gets her way, we'll never speak again.

"Looks like *he's* speaking to *you*," she points out. "Why the deep freeze?"

"You do remember him being a total boor the other day, correct?"

"Vaguely."

I sigh. "Plus, there's the small fact your mother came to my room last night and essentially threatened to have him arrested if I ever see him again."

"WHAT?"

I briefly summarize Octavia's visit to my chambers, leaving

out the part about my wall-punch... and the conversation I had with Carter, afterward.

"Jesus Christ," Chloe mutters when I'm done. "She really has it out for you."

"Any advice?"

"Honestly? Not really. I wish I could tell you this is an idle threat, but... much as it pains me to admit, it might be better for you — and for him — in the long run if you do what she wants."

My expression falls. "You can't honestly think I should cut him out of my life. He's my oldest friend!"

"I can't tell you what to do. I can only tell you about my own experience, going up against Octavia." She grimaces. "In middle school, I made a friend named Kacey. Scholarship kid. Super sweet, dirt poor. We were close... until Octavia decided Kacey's family wasn't a *quality connection* for the stepdaughter of a duke. She told me to end the friendship. I refused." She pulls in a breath. "A week later, Kacey's family abruptly moved away. The official story was that her father got an unexpected transfer at his job to a town six hours from Hightower. Unofficially? It was Octavia. "

"Let me get this straight. She uprooted an entire family across the country, just to prevent you from being friends with some random girl?"

"The fact that she'd walked in on me and Kacey making out in my bed the previous week probably didn't help my case." Chloe winks at me. "Can you *imagine*? The perfect Lancaster image, tarnished by a *lesbian*!?"

"I'm sorry, Chloe. That's..." My head shakes. "That's bull-shit. You should be free to be with whoever the hell you want — free to *be* whoever the hell you want."

"Don't you worry about me. Octavia may not be thrilled that I'm a solid 3 on the Kinsey Scale, but I got my revenge."

Her eyebrows waggle. "Swiss all-girls boarding school, remember?"

I burst out laughing. After a second, she joins in with me.

"You know, I should've said this earlier…" I clear my throat. "I'm really sorry about the other day. Owen usually isn't so… combative."

"You didn't do anything wrong. Don't apologize for him." She sighs. "And, much as I'd like to hold a grudge, in this case I won't. Men are idiots when they're in love."

I blink rapidly. "Excuse me?"

"Oh come on." She glances over at me. "You can't pretend you didn't know."

"You're totally off base, here. There's no way Owen is in love with me. He's my—"

"Best friend. *Riiiiight.* Keep telling yourself that."

"He is!" I insist. "We've never so much as kissed."

"Never?"

"Never."

"Huh. Well. That still doesn't change my assessment," Chloe says stubbornly. "It's the only explanation for all his macho bullshit: he realized he was about to lose you and he flipped out."

"Yes — lose me *as a friend.*"

"A friend he wants to bend over and fuck to kingdom come, perhaps."

"Chloe!"

"What? Don't be such a prude."

"I'm definitely not a prude. I just…" I flush. "I don't like thinking about having sex with Owen. It's weird."

"I'd have sex with him." She whistles wolfishly. "The boy may be an asshole, but he is fine as hell. I would ride him like an escalator."

"Please, spare me the visuals."

"Suit yourself." She chuckles. "So, if blond hotties don't get your engines revving, who does? What's your type? Clean-cut? Silver fox? Sporty? Rock god?"

I mull over the question. The few guys I've ever had sex with were all casual college flings — dark, drunken hook-up sessions in narrow dormitory beds, typically over and done with in a few short minutes. I don't have the nerve to admit to Chloe that I've never had an orgasm. Never even come close, actually. And I'm *definitely* not about to inform her that the only time I've ever felt even a hint of the passion I've read about in my favorite books was in the backseat of an SUV last Friday night, sitting on her brother's lap, the rock hard length of his erection making itself unapologetically known against my ass.

"Come on," Chloe prompts. "*Spill*. Who was the last guy that inspired some hot sexual fantasies?"

With considerable effort, I manage to push Carter's face to the depths of my psyche.

"No one. Honestly."

"You know, you're a terrible liar." Her eyes dance with humor. "Don't worry. We'll work on that before you become the crown princess. You'll need to be able to bluff with the best of them, if you're going to rule someday."

"*Chloe*! Give it up, already."

She just grins at me, totally unapologetic. After a beat, I can't help grinning back.

I've never had a sibling, so I don't have anything to compare it to… but if this is what it's like to have a sister, I have to say…

It doesn't entirely suck.

CHAPTER TWELVE

THE KNOCK SOUNDS SHARPLY on my bedroom door. A riot of butterflies flutters to life inside my stomach.

"One second!" I call breathlessly. "Almost ready!"

I give myself a final once-over in the floor-length mirror, hardly recognizing the girl staring back at me. Between the freshly dyed hair, the sky-high designer heels, and the immaculately tailored black dress that costs more than any other garment that's ever been on my body... I'm a far cry from the girl with overgrown roots in a skimpy crop top who arrived at the Lockwood Estate a week ago.

Hearing Lady Morrell's voice in the back of my head, I straighten my shoulders and lift my chin.

Posture is pertinent! Your spine should be straight as the steady trunk of a rainforest tree, supporting a whole canopy of branches.

I tuck a glossy mahogany curl behind my ear. I haven't seen my hair this color in — god, I don't even know how long. Surprisingly enough, I don't hate it. And though I gave the stylist a hard time last night when she pulled out the scissors, I have to admit that the layered cut is far more flattering for my heart-shaped face than the drab, uniform length I had before.

Smoothing my hands down the front of my dress, I grab my jet clutch purse off the vanity. My hand hovers over my cellphone, but when I see the screen light up with an incoming call — Owen's name flashing in all caps — I decide to leave it behind. No good can come from talking to him, right now... even if keeping him at arm's length is enough to tear my heart in two.

He's safer this way, I tell myself, eyes stinging painfully. *You heard Chloe's story about Kacey. If Octavia would do something like that to her own daughter... she won't think twice about doing it to you.*

My head tilts back to look at the coffered ceiling, a vain attempt to keep the tears at bay. I know I don't have a choice — that shutting him out is the only way to protect him — but that doesn't make it any easier. He's been calling and texting nonstop. He even showed up at the front gates last night, demanding to see me. Or so one of the guards told me, after they'd turned him away.

Apparently the email I sent two days ago requesting space and time to sort through things on my own was not well received.

"That's how you choose to end a twenty year friendship? A bloody email?" Owen snarled on the voicemail he left around midnight, sounding both inebriated and furious. *"For fuck's sake, Ems. I can't believe you could be this cruel."*

Chloe knocks again, harder this time.

"I'm coming, I'm coming!" I mutter, wiping a tear as I head for the door. "Hold your horses, Chl— *Oh!*" My throat convulses as I pull open the door and find myself face to face with Carter, looking utterly incredible in a black suit that hugs every plane of his sculpted body.

Holy fuck.

"You're not Chloe," I breathe stupidly, unable to tear my eyes away from him.

"No," he murmurs in a tight voice. "I'm not."

I nearly stumble back when I see the dangerous heat burning in his eyes. He drinks me in, inch by inch, his gaze dragging slowly up the length of my body from the black stilettos on my feet to the fitted curves of my dress to the dark brown curls falling around my shoulders in an elegant half-up style.

"You look…" he trails off, jaw clenching tight.

"Different?" I supply. "It's the hair."

A muscle jumps in his cheek. "Trust me. It's not the hair."

My fingers grip my clutch purse so hard, I worry I'll snap the clasp as Carter takes a step toward me, closing a sliver of the distance between us. My breath catches, watching his hand lift to gently take one of my curls between his index finger and his thumb — just as he did the first night we met. I stop breathing altogether as his fingers slide down, stretching the lock to its full length.

It's the most erotic touch of my life, and I can't even feel it.

"What are you doing?" I ask breathlessly.

His eyes flicker to mine, molten with banked heat. His mouth opens, he leans in…

"*Hey!*"

We both flinch back at the sound of Chloe's voice. My eyes drop to the hallway floor. Carter clears his throat roughly, turning away from me.

"Let's go, you two!" she calls from the top of the grand staircase, gesturing madly. "The limos are waiting outside. Don't worry — I already made sure we aren't riding with Linus and Octavia."

"Thank god for small miracles," I murmur, looking anywhere but at Carter.

He doesn't say a word as the three of us make our way out

the front doors and down into the driveway, where Octavia and Linus are waiting by the limos with Simms. At least ten of the King's Guard are also present, armed to the hilt — literally, they're all wearing swords — in impressive navy blue military uniforms. Their double-breasted gold buttons gleam brightly in the early morning sunshine. They look more ready to take on an invading army than accompany a grieving family to a funeral.

"Is all this pomp really necessary?" Chloe asks.

"Seeing as someone has recently attacked the crown? *Yes*," Octavia snaps at her daughter. "A certain show of force must be made during our first public appearance."

Linus coughs, a rheumy sound. "Your mother is right."

I meet his eyes and see an unfamiliar expression on his face as he evaluates me.

Could it be pride?

"Emilia," he murmurs. "You look absolutely lovely."

I open my mouth to thank him, but Octavia interrupts shrilly. "Yes, well, *lovely* as she may be, she's delayed us insufferably. We're running quite behind schedule. Everyone — into the cars this instant. We will see you at the Abbey. You won't arrive until shortly after us, as you'll be diverting to Westgate to pick up the Sterling children before the ceremony."

"Oh, *perfect*." Chloe groans dully. I hear Carter sigh deeply from my other side, equally perturbed, and my curiosity magnifies. I'm sure I've heard the name Sterling before, but I can't put my finger on the context.

I shoot Chloe a questioning glance. She mouths the words *I'll explain later*, eyes rolling back in her head.

Octavia, Linus, and Simms climb into the first limo while I follow Chloe and Carter into the second. We settle onto supple seats and I try not to let my awe leak through as I take it all in. I've never ridden in a limousine before, let alone one from the vintage Rolls Royce fleet used by the royal family for all formal events. My eyes scan from the fully stocked bar of glass decanters to the plush carpeted floor to the hand-embroidered royal crest that decorates the privacy partition. Every detail appears custom designed for maximum comfort and style.

We've barely pulled out of the driveway when Chloe reaches into the beaded bodice of her frock and retrieves a rolled joint from her bra. She lights up and takes a deep hit before extending it in my direction.

"No thanks."

"Carter?" she offers, voice scratchy with smoke.

He shakes his head, reaching instead for the decanter of bourbon. Pouring a few fingers into two separate glasses, he takes one for himself and leans forward to hand the other to me.

My fingers close automatically around the smooth crystal. "Oh, I don't think I need—"

"Just sip it," he murmurs, staring into my eyes. I know he can read the emotions churning inside them — all the fear and worry and butterfly-induced nausea. "It'll calm your nerves."

With a nod of appreciation, I take a hesitant sip. He's right. The minute the warm liquid hits my stomach, I feel some of the swarming butterflies dissipate.

The atmosphere is unusually quiet as we roll onward, each of us wrapped up in our own thoughts, enveloped in that unique somberness that accompanies all funeral processions.

"So." I clear my throat and they both look at me. "Who, exactly, are the Sterlings and why do you both hate them?"

Carter snorts and takes another gulp of bourbon.

Chloe giggles. "First of all, we don't hate them. There's just… a lot of complicated history between their family and the Lancasters. Starting with the fact that Ava was engaged to Prince Henry. And her brother Alden was his best friend."

"*Is,*" Carter corrects lowly. "Not *was*. Henry isn't dead, Chloe."

"Really? How would you know, Carter? Last I checked, you haven't even been to see him."

"Don't be a bitch, Chloe."

She flips him off and takes another puff of pot.

"You were out with Ava the night of the fire," I recall as fragments from a previous conversation suddenly click together in my mind. "At a club opening in Lund."

Chloe blows out a perfect ring of smoke, smirking at her own parlor trick. "Yep. Hard to say what she was more upset about — the fact that her chance to be queen legitimately went up in smoke, or that her fiancé had the gall to inhale so much of it during that fire."

"You make it sound as if she doesn't care about him at all."

Chloe shoots Carter an interesting look. "Care to offer an opinion on that, dear brother?"

He takes another gulp of bourbon and stares pointedly out the window.

"So…" My brow creases as I try to sort out the complicated dynamics. "You *aren't* friends, then?"

"We were growing up. All five of us, actually — me, Carter, Henry, Ava, Alden. Thick as thieves."

"And now?"

"Now, Ava and I are more like… frenemies?" She shrugs. "Our families are connected."

"Meaning…"

"Look, E, you're new to all this, so I don't think you realize how small the circle of aristocratic families in Germania is. Even if you don't like someone, it's practically guaranteed you'll cross paths relatively often at charity fundraisers, galas, balls, coronations…"

"Funerals," Carter supplies darkly.

We all go silent again.

"My point is, if I avoided every asshole in this country,

there'd be no one left. *Including* my own flesh and blood," she says glancing briefly at Carter again. "But if you want my advice… just be on your guard around them, okay? Especially once they find out who you really are."

"They *won't*," I insist. "I'm undercover. Your new royal aide, remember?"

"Mhm. But don't be shocked if they figure it out eventually. Ava and Alden have been groomed for this life since infancy. They love nothing better than a juicy piece of gossip, and they know exactly how to use it to their own advantage." Chloe shakes her head. "They play the political game better than anyone I've ever met. Maybe even Octavia. How else do you think a girl gets a crown prince as handsome as Henry to *propose* at the ripe age of twenty-five?"

With Chloe's words tumbling around inside my head, I stare out the tinted window taking slow sips of bourbon to settle my churning stomach. About twenty minutes later, we pull up in front of a stately manor house, half the size of the Lockwood Estate but no less beautiful. Two white-gloved butlers sweep open the imposing carved oak doors as we roll to a stop. I watch, dazzled, as two of the most attractive humans I've ever seen step out into the morning light.

Platinum blond and staggeringly tall, they're the picture of elegance as they descend the steps to the gently sloping driveway where we're idling. Our chauffeur gets out to hold open the limousine door for them. I slide down the leather bench seat to make some room and find myself pressed uncomfortably close to Carter's side.

"Sorry," I murmur.

His Adam's apple bobs roughly. "Don't worry about it."

The Sterling siblings climb into the backseat so gracefully, they remind me of swans settling on the water's surface. He's in solid black — from his suit to his tie to his shirt to his pocket square. Even his cufflinks glitter darkly, crafted from the deepest onyx. She's in an exquisite silk dress and an ornate cocktail hat with a netted veil that dips low to cover one half of her stunning face.

Alden and Carter exchange stiff nods while the girls fawn like old friends.

"Chloe, darling. So good to see you," Ava exclaims, leaning forward to air-kiss Chloe once on each cheek. "How are you holding up?"

"You know me," Chloe drawls, re-lighting her blunt as soon as the greetings are done. She blows out a puff of smoke. "Walking on sunshine."

"Charming." Ava coughs lightly and makes a show of fanning her face with a white-gloved hand. Her light hazel eyes rove around the interior of the limo, lingering for an uncomfortably long time on Carter — or maybe that's just my imagination running wild — before finally sliding over to me. She seems to zero in on the small point of contact where my bare arm brushes up against his suit.

"And who is this new face?" Ava asks tightly.

My mind blanks for a minute as I try to remember my cover story, unexpectedly rattled by the intensity of her stare.

"Oh, her?" Chloe's eyes twinkle with good humor as she interjects. She's actually *enjoying* this, the loon. "No one of consequence. Just my new assistant, Emilia."

"I wasn't aware smoking marijuana all day required assistance." Ava's tone may be prim and proper, but there's no mistaking the bite beneath her words. I'm vastly relieved when her eyes slide away from me.

A lowly assistant isn't worth her attention.

I finish off my bourbon in a single gulp.

"Yes, well we can't all be as productive as you, Ava." Chloe's grin looks more like a grimace. "How many organizations do you co-chair, now? Four?"

"Five. There's the Lund Beautification Society, the City Gardeners Association, the Veterans Relief Fund, the Art Preservation Council, and *of course* the wonderful work we've been doing to save the spotted owl population in the eastern mountains. Were you aware they're endangered? It's so important that we…"

I promptly tune her out, watching Chloe take another drag. Her eyes are glazed, whether from the drugs or the self-inflated chatter is anyone's guess. The more Ava prattles on about her own endeavors, the stranger I find it. She hasn't mentioned her fiancé. Not once. She's acting like we're on our way to a charity fundraiser for her precious spotted owls, not the funeral of two people who were supposed to be her in-laws, someday.

Equally strange is that her brother, Alden, says nothing the entire ride. Not a single word. His jaw is locked tight as he stares out the window, eyes unfocused with either grief or boredom. I can't tell from here.

"…and our focus should really be on restoring the natural grasses and trees that used to grow plentifully in those at-risk areas, because I think we can all agree, without a habitat, there's not even a chance…"

God, does she ever take a breath?

Without a word, Carter grabs the decanter and refills my glass along with his own. Taking a fortifying sip, I tap my elbow against his.

Thank you.

A second later, I smile into my bourbon when his shoulder presses subtly against mine.

You're welcome.

HAVE you ever driven through a crowd of half a million mourners?

I'd imagine it's a lot like the procession at a royal wedding or the celebratory parade after particularly impressive football championship... except, instead of cheers, tears flow freely. Instead of team colors, a sea of black, punctuated by the occasional bolt of blue and gold — a Germanian flag, waving proudly over closed shop-doors and tight-shuttered houses.

Somber citizens line every street from the outskirts of Vasgaard's historic district all the way to Windsor Abbey. They blow kisses, salute, and throw flowers into the path of the twin black hearses that lead our procession — carrying King Leopold and Queen Abigail on one last tour through their capital city.

A final goodbye.

Several limos trail after in a long, stately line, ours second only to the one carrying Linus and Octavia, followed closely by a cluster Chloe would refer to as *the far side of the family tree*. At our creeping pace, it takes nearly two hours to drive from one end of the city to the next. Feeling strangely numb, I stare out at the faces as we pass, safe in the knowledge they can't see me through our tinted windows.

A week ago, I would've been out there with them.

Would've *been* one of them.

Now, I am somewhere else.

Someone else.

When we finally reach the abbey, a towering vision of steeples and stained glass, I catch sight of the photographers lining the security barricades, their telephoto lenses snapping endless shots of Linus and Octavia as they ascend the steps toward the doors in a stately fashion. My heart begins to pound so hard I'm sure Carter can hear it, seated so close beside me. I've never felt more grateful for my anonymity.

Internally, I recite the plan, hoping it'll help calm me.

Stand behind Simms at a respectful distance.
Don't stare, don't fidget, don't draw attention.
No one knows who you are or why you're here.
No one will even take notice of you.

A shuddering breath rattles from my lungs as I feel the brakes engage. It's our turn to disembark.

Ava, Alden, and Chloe scramble out first. Alone in the limo, Carter's eyes cut to mine for the briefest of moments.

"Don't forget to breathe, love."

With that, we step out into the unrelenting gloom of the cold October day.

CHAPTER THIRTEEN

THE CEREMONY ITSELF IS LOVELY.

Lovely, but *long* — hours of benedictions and prayers, scripture and sermon, eulogies and ensemble choirs. By the time we finally filter out of Windsor Abbey, my feet are aching. My heart is heavy. My eyes are damp with tears I didn't think I'd shed for the aunt and uncle I never got to meet.

Goodbye, Leopold and Abigail. I hope you are at peace, now.

Our group has expanded to include Lord and Lady Sterling — Ava and Alden's parents — who are just as pale and tall as their children. They don't bother introducing themselves to me as we make our way down the steps, through a gauntlet of King's Guard in their formal blue uniforms.

I trail close on Simms' heels, keeping my eyes downcast, listening to the muffled click of press cameras from all sides. It's the loudest noise to be heard in the gathered crowd of thousands.

Click, click, click, click.

We're nearly to the bottom of the stairs, where the waiting

limousines offer refuge. For the first time all day, I feel a hint of my anxiety dissipate.

It's over.

My relief is short lived. A shout — slurred with alcohol, but oh so familiar — pierces the air like a clap of thunder in the otherwise silent crowd.

"EMILIA!"

I hear people turning toward the voice, stunned by the man who would dare interrupt such a somber occasion with senseless screaming, but I don't dare look; not with the entire country watching.

"EMILIA LANCASTER!"

The crowd begins to titter, curiosity crashing through the masses like a wave.

Did he say Lancaster?

Simms glances back at me, concern etched on his features. Carter and Chloe do the same. My heart begins to pound as the King's Guard closes rank, hands on their hilts, hurrying us down the remaining steps as fast as possible without causing a scene.

"LOOK AT ME!" Owen's words are garbled, but still intelligible. "EMILIA, YOU CAN'T DO THIS — YOU CAN'T JUST CUT ME OUT! *PLEASE!*"

When his voice cracks, I can no longer control myself. My eyes lift to find him in the crowd — blond hair falling onto his forehead, brown eyes bloodshot. Our gazes connect for a moment, and I shake my head as if to say, *Please, Owen, don't say any more.*

Please, let this go.

Let me go.

His expression crumbles, hope disintegrating into bitter resentment. And I know, even before his mouth opens again, that what comes next will be catastrophic.

"I GUESS TWENTY YEARS OF FRIENDSHIP MEANS

NOTHING, NOW THAT YOU'RE ROYALTY. IS THAT IT, EMS? OR SHOULD I CALL YOU PRINCESS EMILIA, NOW?"

The word *princess* sets off a detonation the likes of which the world has never before seen. The press goes nuclear — a mushroom cloud of outrage and speculation rising up into the sky, the fallout incalculable.

And Owen is ground zero.

I see guards closing in on him, dark looks on their faces as they take him into custody. Simultaneously, I watch as at least two dozen reporters circle him, hurling questions rapid-fire, desperate for his story. Unfortunately, the rest of them — at least three or four hundred, all with voice recorders at the ready — are staring at me.

Correction: screaming at me.

"That's her!"

"Emilia, look this way!"

"Is it true you're the princess?"

"Can you comment on your connection to the Lancaster family?"

My wide eyes swing around as a bombardment of camera flashes blind me. I feel like a bug trapped beneath a magnifying glass, being slowly burned alive.

"King Linus! Is it true? Can you confirm she is your daughter?"

"Is she a legitimate heir?"

"Does Germania have a hidden princess?"

There's a screech of tires as the limo squeals away from the steps, whisking Linus, Octavia, Simms, and the Sterling parents from the scene. The rest of our group hurries toward the second vehicle, but I can't seem to move fast enough to keep up. My feat have turned to anvils on the steps of the abbey.

"Emilia! Look this way! Princess Emilia!"

Emilia!

Emilia!

Emilia!

Suddenly, there's a warm hand on the small of my back and a towering male silhouette shielding me from the crowd. I know it's Carter without looking up at him. Even now, with my senses screaming for relief and my eyes glossed with tears, my body recognizes his.

Somehow, we make it into the limo. The door closes behind us with a slam, cutting off the worst of the screams, but there's no escaping the thundering crowd as they surround us on all sides, frantic to get their photographs even through the tinted glass.

I press my eyes closed with the heels of my hands, as though that will somehow make them disappear. I don't open them again until we're several blocks away, racing out of the city at nearly twice the legal speed limit.

Chloe, Carter, Ava, and Alden are all staring at me, a mix of shock and concern etched on all their faces. To my great surprise, it's Alden — quiet, composed Alden — who finally breaks the silence. His cultured voice is thick with incredulity.

"Anyone care to explain what the actual *fuck* just happened?"

It's a question that will be repeated — with varying amounts of profanity — over and over by every news outlet on the planet in the next few hours. Because from Germania to Gibraltar, America to Argentina, Morocco to Malaysia... everyone's wondering the same thing.

Who is the secret princess?

In a world of social media and twenty-four hour news cycles, it doesn't take long for the rest of the world to piece together the story of Emilia Victoria Lancaster. Or, at least, their shiny, fairy tale version of it.

Ordinary girl becomes royalty overnight!

Chloe, Carter, and I hover in the Lockwood Estate's large conference room, eyes on the television screens, watching my anonymity disappear in slow degrees — one news story after another picking apart every aspect of the girl I used to be.

...twenty years old...

...student at Vasgaard University...

...prestigious clinical psychology internship...

...mother, Nina Lennox, deceased...

...complications following pneumonia...

I'm grateful that the Sterlings aren't here to witness this humiliation. I'm even more grateful that Simms already scrubbed my social media presence from the face of the earth. Not that I was ever a prolific poster, but as far as I'm concerned, the fewer pictures and memories these vultures have to dissect on their morning talk shows, the better.

"It's not so bad," Chloe says, bumping her shoulder against mine as a horrid shot of me with frizzy hair and braces flashes on the screen. My middle school portrait, if I remember correctly.

I glance at her skeptically. "I thought you didn't do bullshit."

She sighs. "Look... it was going to come out eventually, right?"

"No! *Not* right. Not if I didn't want it to." I drop my head into my hands with a groan. "This was supposed to be my decision."

"It still is," she insists.

"No, it's not! Now, the whole world gets a vote."

"Fuck the world."

I look up sharply at the sound of Carter's voice. He's staring at me, brows pulled in, eyes intent.

"What?" I breathe.

"Fuck the world," he repeats. "They can't make you be someone you don't want to be, Emilia. If you don't want this...

no one can force you into it. Not the press, not Linus, not even that jackass boyfriend of yours."

"He's not my boyfriend. He's not even my friend. Not anymore." My voice cracks pathetically — a faint hint at the fissure of betrayal that's opened up inside me, so deep I cannot seem to find my way out. "But… thank you anyway. For saying that."

He nods gravely.

I look back at the television, where a series of video clips and images are playing on a constant loop. The news anchor gleefully freeze-frames my frozen panic on the Windsor Abbey steps, then zooms in until the fear in my eyes is magnified large enough to fill the whole screen. I want to tear my gaze away, but I can't.

"The royal family has yet to issue an official statement, but we are hearing word that the palace press secretary, Gerald Simms, will be in touch before the day ends…" The newswoman shuffles the papers on her desk. "We take you now to our correspondent on the ground, Sara Wertz, who is reporting live from outside the Hawthorne home where the princess grew up…"

I suck in a breath when the screen flashes with a live feed of my house, its chipped paint and crooked shutters rather a dull sight. There are several King's Guard positioned around the perimeter… along with about a hundred members of the press, all desperate for a scoop.

It's a total mob scene.

My heart lurches in my chest when the familiar face of my neighbor appears, a microphone shoved toward her mouth.

"Ma'am, care to answer any questions about the princess? Is it true she grew up right across the street?"

Before I can hear whether or not sweet old Mrs. Carmichael is about to sell me out to the press, Carter strides angrily toward the television and switches it off with such violence, I'm surprised it doesn't crash to the floor.

In the heavy silence that follows, my eyes burn into the now-black screen where, if I squint, I can just make out the silhouette of the strange girl staring back at me. The one with dark brown hair and a broken spirit.

The side door opens with a soft creak. Simms steps in, his expression grave.

"Your Highness," he murmurs, and for the first time, I don't bother correcting him. "The king is asking for you."

♛

FOR NEARLY A FULL minute Linus just stares at me, hands steepled in front of him on his vast desk. I try not to be intimidated, jerking my chin up and holding his eyes.

"Today did not go as planned," he says finally.

"No," I agree. "I'm sorry. The funeral…"

"What happened was not your fault. Still, certain reparations must be made. To that end, we will be holding a press conference tomorrow morning, officially announcing you as my heir. I would like you to be there, at my side, when we make the announcement. As a show of strength."

He waits for my response.

I don't offer one.

"Now that the funeral is behind us, we will be moving into the castle to officially mark the beginning of my reign." He pauses again. "The East Wing is traditionally reserved for the heir apparent but, naturally, it is not currently available due to the fire. For the time being, you will occupy a suite in the North Wing, along with Chloe and Carter."

I refrain from commenting.

"Eventually, we will restore the palace to its former glory. But we don't want to appear too hasty in rebuilding. Not with Henry still…" he trails off.

140

I clench my jaw tighter.

The silence grows suffocating.

"*Emilia.*" He sighs, as though I'm being terribly tiresome. "I know you were hoping to avoid this outcome for a few more weeks, but we must face facts. The situation has changed. You no longer have the liberty of a choice in this matter. *You are the Crown Princess of Germania.* It is your birthright and your responsibility. And tomorrow, the whole world will watch as you finally accept it."

I clear my throat, making sure I have control over my volume before I attempt to respond. "So everything you said — everything you promised me before, about how I'd get to decide my own path… that was all bullshit?"

He leans back in his chair. "It was not *bullshit.* It was me, attempting to extend your childish illusion of freedom for a little while longer. A kindness, if you will."

"A *kindness?*" I scoff bitterly. "You're joking."

"I do not have the luxury of making jokes. Not today."

"If this is how you treat your family, I'd love to know how handle your enemies."

"Disobey me and perhaps you shall," he threatens in a hard tone.

"Wow. You're a real piece of work, you know that?"

"Be that as it may, I am also a *king* with the weight of an entire country on my shoulders. Like it or not, your desires are not the only ones in Germania that concern me." His eyes turn to emerald chips of ice. "Which is why you *will* be at that press conference tomorrow. You *will* act in a dignified manner. And you *will* verbally acknowledge your intent to take up the role of crown princess."

"And if I don't?"

He weighs his words carefully for a moment. "Then your house in Hawthorne goes on the market. I imagine, now that people know their princess once lived there, it will sell quite quickly."

"You can't do that," I gasp. "You've already paid off the mortgage! The house is mine, free and clear."

"Is it?"

My blood runs cold. "What?"

He leans across the table toward me. "You see, I had a feeling we might run into a snag like this one at some point down the line. That's why, instead of paying the bank the full amount owed in your name... I paid it in mine. Which means I now control a significant lien on your property."

"But I still have the deed," I insist, hardly believing my ears.

"If you research property law, you will find that the deed ceases to matter at a certain point — usually once your mortgage payments lapse and you fail to pay your property taxes." His expression softens slightly. "For all intents and purposes, I have assumed all financial responsibility for your home, Emilia. It's mine. And if you choose to walk away from your duty... You will have nowhere left to go."

I go completely still, feeling that fault line of betrayal deep inside me open even wider. First Owen, now Linus.

How much treachery can one heart take in a single day?

Naively, I handed over the thing that matters most, in the vain belief that he would honor his word and safeguard it. Instead, he's using it to control me.

What a fool I was, to trust this man. To fall for the fairy tale, despite every atom in my body screaming I should do otherwise.

Did you forget there was a reason Mom hated him?

I thought, deep down, there might still be some sliver of paternal loyalty inside Linus' soul. I see now how grave an error that was. He doesn't give a shit about me. He doesn't give a shit about anyone or anything except himself, his crown, and his legacy.

Ironically enough, it's Octavia's words I hear in this moment.

The only person Linus Lancaster serves is Linus Lancaster. You will find out for yourself just how little you matter to him, as soon as your interests stop aligning with his own.

She warned me this would happen, but I was either too stupid or too stubborn to listen to her. And as I sit there in my father's office, feeling my careful plans fall to pieces, I nearly laugh at how artfully I have been outmaneuvered in this game we're all playing.

It's almost absurd: after today, the whole world thinks I'm royalty.

But I'm not a princess.

I'm a pawn.

CHAPTER FOURTEEN

I WIND up right back where I first started — sitting in the dark on a cold stone bench in a forgotten garden. My eyes are wet. My heart is empty.

At least it's not raining, this time.

I've come full circle in the span of a week.

God, has it truly only been a week?

Everything's changed so fast, from the scope of my future right down to the color of my hair. It's hard to believe ten days ago, I was a regular girl on my way to class. My biggest worries consisted of midterm grades and whether the cute guy in my pharmacology lecture was flirting with me or just being friendly when he asked to go over our notes together after class.

I had a best friend. I had a home. I had a career path.

And now… I have no one.

Nothing.

Just a title I don't want and a bottomless abyss of anguish swirling inside me like a black hole.

The tears drip faster, even when I arch my neck to stare up at the stars. Halfheartedly, I pick out a few constellations as I shiver and shake in my pretty black dress.

Ten minutes go by.

I wait.

Twenty.

I wait.

Thirty.

Forty.

Fifty.

I wait.

I wait.

I wait.

Because I think… some part of me knows he'll come, even before he makes the conscious choice to leave the manor, far before I hear his voice in the darkness at my back.

"I see you're back to your original plan."

Carter.

My throat convulses. I don't turn to look at him. I can't. Not yet. Not with my face a mess of tears.

There's a crunch of gravel as he walks up behind me. A second later, my shoulders are enveloped by warm fabric — his suit jacket, settling around me like a blanket. My fingers latch onto the lapels as his lips brush my ear.

"I thought we already ruled out you dying of exposure to avoid becoming the princess," he murmurs.

I try to find words, but my throat is clogged by tears and grief and something else. Something I'm not ready to name, just yet.

Carter sits down on the bench beside me. He's so close, the heat of his strong thigh seeps into mine. I slide my arms inside his sleeves and try not to notice how much better I feel, just being near him.

"Emilia… are you okay?"

"No," I croak. "No, I'm really not."

145

"Is there anything…" He blows out a breath, as if he's not sure how to say this properly. "Can I do anything to make this better for you?"

"You don't happen to have a time machine?"

"Afraid not."

"Cloak of invisibility?"

His head shakes.

"Then, no, Carter. I think I'm on my own."

His hands curl around the stone bench seat. He's practically thrumming with anger and frustration.

"It's actually pretty funny," I tell him in a hollow voice that isn't funny at all. "I'm a psychology student. I study human behavior. I read all these books about our capacity for manipulation and evil. About every atrocity we, as a species, have committed against one another over tens of thousands of years. How we've actually *evolved* to be cruel and self-serving, rather than honest and true." I pull in a shallow breath. "All that knowledge, right there at my fingertips… and still, I'm totally blindsided when it happens to me."

"Emilia…" My name catches in his throat.

"Why did he do it?" I ask, another tear trickling out. "He's my best friend. I'd do anything to protect him — even cut him out of my life when I need him most. But he… he decided to hurt me in the precise way he knew would inflict the most damage. *How could he do that to me?*" I feel like my heart has been ripped right out of my chest, leaving only a gaping hole behind. "And Linus… Linus…"

I can't even begin to get the words out.

"Emilia, please look at me."

I shake my head, still crying, and use his sleeve to mop the tears off my cheeks. "You should go. Just… leave me alone."

"*No.*"

"I'm not good company at the moment, Carter."

"I don't give a shit. I'm not good company *ever*. But we all need someone sometimes. Someone to lean on." He's breathing hard. I can hear the rapid rise and fall of his chest as he watches me weep. "If you need to lean on someone tonight... I'll be here."

My breath hitches on a sob.

He's whispering, now. Barely audible. "I'm here, love."

It's the *love* that breaks me. My head turns toward him and our eyes lock in the span of a heartbeat. And on any other night, I'd try to fight it — that magnetic tug I feel whenever I'm around him. But I don't have any more fight left in me.

I gaze into his beautiful face, at the heartbreaking contradiction of tenderness and fear playing out on those gorgeous goddamned features, and I can't stop myself from falling forward into his chest.

His arms come around me, crushing me to him. It's not like our last hug — there's no uncertainty, no hesitation. This one is fierce, fraught with need. The need to touch and cling to a man who isn't going to rip the rug out from under me. At least, not right now.

I press my wet eyes against the column of his throat and hear him inhale sharply. My hands wind around his broad shoulders, then slide up to lace behind his neck as I flatten myself against him — chest to chest, heart to heart. And it's totally crazy... but there, with our pulses racing in time to the same beat, I think that Carter might just be strong enough to bear the weight of dark despair inside me. Even if it's only for a few minutes.

We stay like that until my tears have slowed and my choppy breaths have leveled out. Feeling blessedly numb for the first time in hours, I lift my head to look at him.

Our faces align perfectly in the darkness. My fingers grip the back of his neck, where his hair curls slightly at the nape. A low sound rattles deep inside his throat — whether to warn me away or urge me closer, I'm not certain. His blue eyes burn so hot, flames of desire dance along my skin as I lean in, inch by careful inch. And before I can talk myself out of it…

I brush my lips against his.

It's meant to be chaste. A simple thank you. That's what I tell myself, anyway. But that small brush sparks into something else — something that soon blazes out of my control.

Carter's hands lift to cup my tear-swollen face… my fingertips dig tight against the back of his neck… and quite suddenly, with no warning at all, he's kissing me.

Or maybe I'm kissing him.

I'm not sure who moves first.

I'm not sure it matters.

The only thing I know with certainty is, now that it's happening, there's no turning back. Never mind that it's wrong. Forbidden. Doomed. Never mind that it never should've happened.

A brush. A spark.

A kiss. A wildfire.

We are an inferno. A combustible, uncontrollable flame. With a hungry groan, his tongue spears into my mouth — teasing, tasting, consuming — and I can't help the cry that tears from my throat.

Yes.

God, yes.

I didn't realize how much I craved his touch until I felt his big hands moving over my skin. How much I wanted this — his grip sliding back into my hair, his teeth nipping at my bottom lip, his hard body flush against mine.

Or, maybe I did realize, I just didn't acknowledge it. Not even to myself, except in the darkest corners of my mind when I'd replay that first night we met. That spark I felt, even then, when we were two strangers in the backseat of an SUV, without any names or futures or families to hold us back.

The kiss turns desperate, ravenous. We cling tightly, a rising tide of passion sweeping us both away until any chance of turning back is lost to the undertow. His hands slide down my body, exploring the curves of my waist, searching for any exposed patch of skin he can caress. I try to maneuver myself onto his lap but my damn dress is so tight, it's impossible to straddle him. Rife with impatience, Carter reaches down to the side slit of my skirt and promptly tears it from upper-calf to upper-thigh. My eyes go wide at the sound of fabric ripping as he does the same to the other side.

A second later, I no longer care that he's reduced my dress to ribbons, because he pulls me down onto his lap. My knees hit the stone bench on either side of his thighs as I plant myself firmly against him. A bolt of pure, unadulterated lust shoots straight between my legs as I feel the evidence of his desire for me — his long, hard cock, throbbing with need even through the fabric of his pants.

"God, Emilia," he groans against my neck, gripping me so hard it's almost painful. I clutch him back just as tight, grounding myself in his touch. Needing to feel something besides grief and sadness and heartache. But even as he holds me steady, I'm spinning out of control. I can feel it happening, and I'm powerless to stop it.

A shout in a silent crowd.

A thousand camera flashes.

A cruel knife to the back.

I kiss him harder, hoping it'll block the memories I don't want to see, the emotions I don't want to feel. I need him to take hold of me until my world makes sense again, to touch me until I forget everything that's happened since I came to this godforsaken place.

Octavia.

Linus.

Owen.

He nips along my jawline, kissing and biting and teasing his way back to my mouth. I revel in the harsh press of his fingers against my back as our lips tangle together again. Some twisted part of me hopes he leaves marks on my skin, so tomorrow when I wake up, I have proof this wasn't some fragment of a dream.

In my head, I know being with Carter is dirty and broken and wrong. But somehow, as he lowers me backward onto the stone bench, he's the only thing in my whole horrible life that feels totally, completely *right*. My body is a lit fuse, every nerve ending sizzling as his weight comes down on top of me.

I need him.

I need this.

To feel dominated by my choice, not by someone else's design.

There's a certain sort of beauty in submission. At least, in the kind Carter is slowly inflicting on me with each sweep of his tongue, each stroke of his hands. I am coming undone beneath him, unraveling into something I hardly recognize.

Maybe if he touches me long enough, I'll fade into him.

Cease to exist at all.

Just a memory of a girl on a cold stone bench.

I arch up against him, totally lost in his touch. He gazes down at me and I see a flicker of something in his eyes — not lust, not need.

Concern.

"Emilia," he whispers, pulling back a fraction.

I try to grab him, to crush his lips to mine again until the world blurs out of focus, but he's too strong.

"Kiss me," I plead, voice ragged with desire and despair.

"But you're crying."

"It doesn't matter."

He sits up, pulling me with him. His brows tug inward as his big hands squeeze my biceps. "What do you mean, it doesn't matter? Of course it matters."

"No. It really doesn't." I try to kiss him again, but he's holding me at arm's length. It pisses me off. "Jesus Christ, Carter, don't you get it? Nothing I do makes a damn bit of difference in the outcome of this game. *Nothing matters.* None of this. Not you, not me, not us."

He flinches like I've struck him, but I barely notice. A dam inside me has broken and all my darkness is spilling out in one great flood.

"*None. Of. It. Matters.* Not my father. Not my best friend. Not my house. Not my future. Not even my damn memories, 'cause they took those too. *Tune in to your local news tonight at five for the Emilia Lancaster show!* Learn how her date stood her up for the senior prom! Hear neighbors talk about her tragic teen years! Then, at primetime, we'll delve deep into her mother's agonizing death!"

He's breathing hard, staring at me like he doesn't even recognize me.

"Stop looking at me like that," I say, feeling something crumble inside me. Another fault line, this one made of broken dreams and bad intentions.

"How exactly am I looking at you, Emilia?"

My voice is a shaky whisper. "Like I'm scaring you."

"You *are* scaring me," he murmurs. "Guess what? I'm still here. I'm right fucking here."

He reaches for me, but now I'm the one pulling away — out of his grip, off the bench, onto my feet. My eyes are stinging again and suddenly, everything feels a bit out of focus. Like maybe that swirling black hole of grief inside me has pulled me off balance, out of alignment. I'm on a new orbit now, about to crash into something hard enough to do permanent damage.

To me and to him.

Snap out of it, Emilia… before you make an even bigger mess of things.

Cold air washes over my skin. Like waking up from a dream, the past few minutes flash through my mind, sharp-edged details tearing like knives. Horror wells inside me as the haze of lust clears completely from my head. I stagger backward, as far away from him as I can get without leaving the clearing, a hand pressed over my mouth.

What have I done?

What have we done?

"I'm sorry. I shouldn't have… *I'm sorry,*" I whisper, staring at his expression. Poignant vulnerability, so contrary to his typical callous smirk. Seeing it nearly sends my to my knees. I want to walk over to him, to take his face between my hands and kiss him until I'm lost all over again.

But I don't.

I can't.

"This…" Haltingly, I force myself to say the words — words that feel so incredible wrong. "This was a mistake."

He pushes to his feet and starts toward me, eyes flashing. "Emilia—"

"No, Carter." My head shakes. "*We can't.*"

He stops short, jaw locked tight, and growls, "We already did."

"And it was a mistake! We should… we should just… forget it ever happened."

His face flattens in an instant, turning to the mask of indifference I'm oh so familiar with. The heat in his eyes morphs into frost.

"You could honestly do that?" he asks in a subzero whisper. "You could forget? Just like that?"

I avert my eyes, so ashamed of myself I can't even look at him.

"*I have to.*"

My voice breaks. There's a sob gathering at the back of my throat and I'm not sure how much longer I can contain it. Not waiting for him to respond, I turn and run down the path, my torn skirt flapping around my legs. It's not till I'm back in my bedroom with the door locked that I realize I'm still wearing his suit jacket. Without taking it off, I curl into a ball of misery on my bed and cry myself to sleep.

CHAPTER FIFTEEN

EVERY LITTLE GIRL dreams of living in a castle.

Even me.

Perhaps *especially* me, given my particular family history.

But now that I actually live in one, I wish I could go back and tell my five-year-old self to dream about something better. Not to waste her wishes on a cold, stone keep full of winding corridors and drafty bed chambers.

Then again, my perception could be *slightly* skewed, given the fact that I am, for all intents and purposes, a prisoner here at the lovely Waterford Palace. True, my prison cell is a massive suite done up in peaches-and-cream silks and ornate gold fixtures, with a terrace that overlooks the courtyard... But a cage is still a cage, even if it comes with a king-sized bed, high speed internet, a soaking tub, and a perpetually stocked mini-fridge.

The whole Lancaster clan moved here from the Lockwood Estate the day of the press conference — the same day I stood in front of the world, smiling like an idiot, and declared myself royalty.

All hail Her Royal Highness Emilia Victoria Lancaster, Crown Princess of Germania.

Surrounding me on all sides during this painful interlude was my beloved family: Linus, the father I've always dreamed of; Octavia, the loving stepmother who instantly embraced me as her own; and my wonderful siblings, with whom I've bonded so quickly, you'd think we shared actual blood ties.

Oh! Wait.

No.

That's total bullshit.

Apparently, the press is fond of bullshit, though, because that's the story they've been reporting for the past two weeks. I swear to God, if I read one more glowing portfolio about the Lancaster family and my newfound place in it, I'm going to tear my own hair out by the roots.

That would certainly get their attention.

I wish I could say things have calmed down, but I'd be lying. The interview requests are nonstop — Simms is still fielding at least twenty a day — and the paparazzi are so out of control, I've been confined to the palace until further notice. For my own protection, of course.

Cue eye rolling.

The press merely provides Linus with the perfect excuse to keep me locked away until his coronation next week. Preparations are in full swing; there must be fifty staff here at any given time, working to get the castle ready for the official crowning ceremony as well as the formal ball that will take place immediately afterward.

With the exception of the brief press conference, the coronation will mark my first official public appearance. I'll be on full display, mingling with actual members of the aristocracy, stumbling my way through the steps of the traditional Germanian waltz, and generally just trying not to make a complete fool of myself. To say the thought gives me heart palpitations would be an understatement.

According to Chloe, my worry is unnecessary. In her mind, the only thing that truly matters is my outfit.

I'm telling you, E — you could call the Prime Minister a cabbage-brained cuckold and go on to rule peacefully for fifty years. But if you show up in a puce gown with last season's shoes... they'll never let you live it down.

Thus, the royal dressmakers have been here practically every day to take measurements. I endeavor to keep still as they hold up different fabric swatches against my skin tone, then do my best not to trip as they try out shoe options from a vast array of high heels — as if anyone is even going to see my feet under the mammoth ballgown they're designing.

I don't have the heart to tell them that no matter how hard they try to make me look the part of a perfect princess, I'll never be able to maintain the illusion for an entire evening. Putting a shiny paint job on a rust-bucket only fools people from afar. One glance under the hood, there's no hiding the truth.

Chloe assures me she'll stay by my side for the entire event to help me navigate the crowds. I think this has less to do with self-lessness than it does the long list of eligible bachelors who will be in attendance, all hoping for a piece of Emilia-flavored pie — *her* words, not mine. Princes, barons, dukes, and earls from several neighboring monarchies are flying in for the elegant affair. Apparently, I'm a hot commodity now that I'm to inherit control of one of Europe's most prosperous countries.

Because nothing screams romance like a man who cares more about the crown sitting on your head than the thoughts occurring inside it.

When I remarked on this potential partner flaw, Chloe just shrugged and told me there was no point squandering my good years being single and celibate, so I might as well enjoy the princess perks while they last. A fair point... though the thought of pursuing anything remotely romantic right now is a hard pill to swallow.

Maybe I'd be more inclined to date if not for the slight complication who happens to reside in the suite directly beside mine and goes by the name of Carter. I shoot a glance toward our shared wall, sighing deeply.

He hasn't been here in days, from the sound of it — or, *lack* of sound, I should say. He also hasn't spoken to me since our night in the garden. Not a word, even on the rare occasions we pass each other in the halls or find ourselves in the same room. It's no accident, either. He's actively avoiding my presence.

Last week, while exploring the library — by far the coolest room in the entire castle, with soaring ceilings and so many books it would take two lifetimes to read them all — I came around a corner and found him sprawled in an elegant wingback chair, reading a copy of Oscar Wilde's 'The Picture of Dorian Gray' by one of the roaring fireplaces. For a moment, I just stood there looking at him — the flickering light of the flames dancing on his face, the lock of dark hair falling over his furrowed brow, the elegant lines of his tall frame.

I must've made some small sound — half gasp, half sigh — because he looked up and spotted me hovering there between the shelves, clutching a first edition of 'Rebecca' by Daphne Du Maurier tight against my chest. Without so much as a hello, he snapped his book shut, stood, and strode out of the library.

He did not look back.

That night, the pages of my book were blotchy with falling teardrops.

I'm not completely naive: I did realize, after what happened between us, that things would be strained. But I thought with enough time, the ache inside me would fade; that I'd stop waking in the night, heart pounding from the fragmented images inside my dreams.

My hands in his hair, his tongue in my mouth, his cock pulsing between my thighs.

When I'm awake, I can shut out the memories… but my unconscious mind follows no such practices of self-preservation. Each night is a fresh reminder, unearthing the passion I'm so desperate to bury.

His touch haunts me. I long for it with a need that terrifies me, crave it like a junkie thoroughly addicted after just one fix… no matter how many times I tell myself to let him go.

It never should've happened.

And it never will again.

That night in the garden, I was a certifiable mess — a fraying nerve of pain that needed an outlet. *Carter* became that outlet. He absorbed my damage like a steel drum containing a detonation. He traced my skin with his hands and soothed all my jagged edges. And I let him.

Not just *let* him…

Eagerly encouraged.

Actively participated.

I try not to let myself think too hard about the fact that his room has been empty for the past three days. That someone else out there is probably *actively participating* at this exact moment.

Whoever Carter Thorne spends his time with is none of my business.

With a sigh, I pick up the touch-screen tablet that controls all the settings in my suite, from lighting to housekeeping requests to thermostat to speaker volume. I adjust the temperature, bumping the heat up by a few degrees. There's an undeniable chill in the air that hints at the coming winter. October is slipping away already, the ever-shortening days punctuated by breezy afternoons that kick up leaves into colorful vortexes. On warmer days, I sit out on my terrace watching them spin around the courtyard, but today I'm bundled in an ultra soft cashmere sweater with the doors and windows shut tight.

I press another button and the strains of a familiar song begin to drift though my overhead speakers: *Everybody Wants to Rule the World* by Lorde. It's become somewhat of a personal anthem these past two weeks, bolstering me even in my darkest moments when the castle walls start closing in around me.

Welcome to your life, there's no turning back...

I close my textbook with a bang and stretch my arms overhead with a low groan. Four straight hours of psychopharmacology definitely warrants a study break. My eyes are tired, but it feels good to be focused on real lessons again. Learning something that actually matters instead of the proper curtsey height or the steps to some tedious waltz.

Sorry Lady Morrell.

She still drops by each day, putting her best efforts into making me a proper princess. I force a smile on my face and go through the motions, but I think we both know my heart is no longer in it. Any incentive I had to please Linus with my progress went away the minute I learned that he'd already sealed my fate. Stolen my future. Seized even the illusion of free will from my grasp without an ounce of remorse.

It's strange — you do not fully appreciate the freedom of choice until it is snatched away from you like breath from your lungs after a sharp fall. You take your future for granted as you do the presence of stars in the sky up above you each night. All those endless possibilities stretching out into infinity, each brighter than the last.

But when the clouds pull in and the galaxies fade from the view of your faulty mortal eyes... you find yourself alone in the prison of your own darkness, inconsequentially trapped by a circumstance far beyond your own conception.

A captive in moonless haze.

A shackled girl in a shining crown.

Recognizing the pessimistic spiral of my own thoughts, I force myself to leave my bedroom and seek out a distraction. Namely: *Chloe.* After an hour-long search that includes her private suite, the kitchens, the stables, the throne room, and the library, I finally locate her in the least likely location — inside the glass greenhouse at the center of the courtyard, sitting cross-legged on the slate floor amongst the many flowering pots, an electric yellow bong resting in her hands.

"Yo," she says when I walk in, her voice scratchy from smoke.

I plunk myself down beside her. "What are you doing in the greenhouse? It took me forever to find you."

She shrugs. "No one ever comes out here — especially not Octavia. She'd never risk getting dirt on her perfect designer wardrobe."

I look pointedly at the Louboutin boots on her feet, their cherry red soles on full display.

"Yeah, I know. Pot, meet kettle." She smirks. "But *I* don't mind getting a little dirty. That's the difference."

She takes a big hit from the bong before extending it my way.

I shake my head. "Can't. I have more studying to do later."

"You've spent the past two weeks with your head buried in those books." She squints at me curiously. "Almost like you're trying to avoid something."

"What!? No, I'm not." My heart pumps harder. "I'm just trying to catch up on everything I've missed these past few weeks. Thankfully, my professors were very understanding when I contacted them about make-up assignments."

Chloe snorts. "Um, *obviously*. They're not going to give a

failing grade to their bloody princess. You could probably blow off the rest of your semester and still graduate with honors."

"That's not the point." I sigh tiredly. "I actually *like* psychology. I *like* learning. I *like* reading case studies and going over treatment options."

"Nerd."

"Yes. I am. Unapologetically."

"Not to be harsh, but I still don't see why you're bothering. You'll be a bit busy running a country — I doubt you'll find much occasion to use your degree. " She pauses. "Unless it's to confirm Octavia's narcissistic personality disorder, but I'm not sure we really need a bonafide doctor's diagnosis, for that."

I laugh, but it's unconvincing. I know Chloe is right: I'll never practice psychology. I'll never help anyone. I'll never have any career at all, except the one that comes with a crown attached.

"I guess part of me is just too stubborn to let it go, when I'm so close to finishing," I murmur. "If I do... it feels like I'm conceding to Linus. Like he's broken me completely."

She raises her bong in solidarity. "Stick it to the man, sister."

My laugh is genuine, this time. "Plus, there's the fact that without my studies, I'd be bored out of my skull. There's not much else to do around here."

"That, I will agree with. No amount of drugs can make this place interesting."

"At least *you* get to leave."

"With a full contingent of body guards," she grumbles.

"I'd take the whole damn King's Guard if it meant a few hours outside this castle."

She bumps her shoulder into mine. "It won't be this way forever. After the coronation, the press will simmer down. The story will fade from the headlines. And eventually, investigators will discover who started the fire, and these insane security protocols will ease up. You'll be free to live a normal life. Well... as close to normal as life for a Lancaster ever gets."

I glance over my shoulder, toward the East Wing. Or... the eyesore that used to be the East Wing. It's gone, now; reduced to a pile of blackened ash, the larger pieces of debris already cleared away by a work crew in the night.

"What if they never find out who did it?" I whisper, throat tight.

"They will. They *have* to."

"How do you know?"

"Because the public demands justice for King Leopold and Queen Abigail. They would never stand for this kind of treachery going unpunished. Especially not with Henry's life still hanging in the balance."

"Any word on his condition?"

"No improvement." She takes another bong hit. "I tried to visit him at the hospital yesterday, but they wouldn't let me in."

"Why?"

"He's in a sterile room because of his burns." She shakes her head. "The risk of infection is so high, the doctors say any exposure to outside germs could be fatal, at this point. He's too weak to fight. I think we all know... he's fading more and more each day. It won't be long, now."

"*Dammit.*" My heart lurches. "You know, it's strange: he's my cousin and I've never even met him. Now, he might be dying... and I'll probably never get the chance."

"You'd like him. Everyone does." She pauses for a long moment. "I actually bumped into Alden at the hospital. Just sitting in the waiting room, staring off into space. He looked like he'd been there all day."

"He and Henry were pretty close, right?"

"Best friends. Damn near inseparable, especially after Henry and Ava's engagement. He's taking this really hard. Much harder than that selfish sister of his. She doesn't seem to give a flying fuck about her fiancé dying."

"Then why the engagement?"

She looks at me like I'm an utter idiot. "Ava Sterling would marry a limp-dicked old bullfrog for the chance to be queen someday."

"Ah."

I always forget most people actually *want* to be royal. To them, being one of the Lancasters is a dream to aspire to... not a nightmare to avoid at all costs.

Chloe clears her throat. "Anyway, Alden actually asked me about you."

My brows go up. "Really?"

"Yeah. Wanted to know how you were coping with all this craziness. I told him to swing by the castle and ask you himself."

"*Chloe.*"

"What?" She smiles innocently.

"Please don't try to play matchmaker."

"I'm doing no such thing."

I stare at her doubtfully.

"Honestly! My intentions are pure." She grimaces. "He's lonely and sad, you're lonely and sad... This way you can be lonely and sad *together.*"

"Uh huh. No other reasons?"

"Nope." Her lips twitch. "Though you must admit... the man isn't exactly a chore to look at..."

"Ugh! I knew this was a set up!"

"Oh, come on, E — you're stubborn, but you're not blind. Alden looks like... well, like one of the archangels fell off the ceiling of the Sistine Chapel and wandered north."

I roll my eyes. "So?"

"*So,* weren't you just complaining about being bored out of your mind? This is what I'd call... a creative solution to that problem. In my experience, there's nothing like a toe-curling orgasm to change your whole outlook." Her eyes narrow. "Unless there's some reason you can't go out with him. Something you're not telling me."

My teeth sink into my bottom lip.

Dammit.

The last thing I want to do is hang out with Alden. Between Carter avoiding me like the plague and Owen stalking me via apologetic voicemail messages, the men in my life are already far too complicated. I certainly don't need to add *more* testosterone to that equation. But I'm not sure how to make Chloe understand that without revealing other details I'd rather keep to myself.

"Look, I'm sure he's very nice," I hedge. "If he happens to swing by in a few weeks, maybe I can make time to see him, but—"

"Great! He's coming over tonight at six."

I gasp. "*Chloe!*"

"What?"

"Tell me you're joking!"

"I could, but that would be a lie."

"You're a monster, you know that?!"

She's totally unperturbed, smiling as she flips her thumb against her lighter and watches it flame to life. "Did I mention it's five thirty right now?"

"WHAT?!

"Yeah. Do you plan to wear that on your date?"

Date?!

In a sudden panic, I glance down at myself.

There's a coffee stain on my cashmere sweater and the loose-fitting pair of boyfriend jeans I'm wearing look like something I found in the reject pile of a thrift shop. There are frumpy sheep-skin slippers on my feet. Not an ounce of makeup on my face.

Hair piled atop my head in a messy bun. Bright blue manicure—*sorry, Lady Morrell, I'm a rebel* — chipping off most of my nails.

Basically, I look homeless.

"I hate you," I hiss at Chloe, scampering to my feet and taking off like a bullet.

"Go get 'em, tiger!" she calls after me. I can hear her laughing like a damn hyena even as I barrel out of the greenhouse and head straight for my suite.

CHAPTER SIXTEEN

"Wow," I breathe, turning in a slow circle.

"Told you." Alden's smile is small but genuine. "Nothing beats this view."

He's right. I lean forward on the turret, brush a windswept curl out of my face, and squint my eyes toward the horizon. From up here, the Alps look so close I could practically reach out and touch them. All of Vasgaard is spread out in the valley beneath us, a colorful carpet of red slate roofs and smoking chimneys. The Nelle River snakes along like a brown garden snake, its many bends and stone bridges a striking sight from this vantage.

When Alden showed up at my bedroom door a half hour ago and volunteered to show me his favorite spot in the castle, I must admit I was skeptical. I assumed he'd bring me to the Great Hall, with its vaulted ceilings and gold-gilded throne... or the armory, to fawn over the impressive collection of medieval weaponry... or the stables, to butter me up with the help of a few glossy-eyed horses.

Instead, he led me down the hall to a massive wall tapestry

bearing the double-headed Lancaster lion crest. Pulling an ornate key from his pocket, he pushed the thick fabric aside and proceeded to unlock a narrow door I never knew existed.

Trust me, he said, holding out his hand. *It's worth it.*

Wide-eyed, I placed my hand in his strong, warm grip, then followed him down a dim, cobwebbed hallway. We passed through another door into a pitch-black spiral stairwell, its stone steps worn smooth over hundreds of years. Up, up up we climbed, only the light of Alden's cellphone to illuminate the ascent, until we reached top of the tallest turret of Waterford Palace.

To be honest, I'd began to doubt any view could possibly be worth the burning in my thighs after three hundred steps... but as soon as we stepped through the thick wooden door into the small round spire, I forgot about my sore muscles.

The view from up here is, quite simply, incredible.

"I didn't even know people could come up here," I say, awed. "I thought it was sealed off years ago."

"Not sealed, per se. Just... discouraged from public use. It's not on the sanctioned castle tour, that's for sure. "

I move to the other side of the tower, eyes fixed on distant skies. "Will they throw us in the dungeons for trespassing, then?"

He laughs. "You? Certainly not. You're the princess. Technically, you own this turret. *Me*, on the other hand..."

"Don't worry. I'll use my vast authority to free you."

"How very benevolent of you, Your Royal Highness." Teasing me, he bows low at the waist, wrist flourishing in a well-practiced gesture. It's so smoothly done, I can't help smiling. Genuinely smiling. For the first time in weeks.

I'm stunned to find I'm actually enjoying myself. It's so good to be out of my room, standing on top of the world with a hand-some man who isn't at all complicated, who doesn't make my head spin with torturous thoughts or my heart race with treacherous feelings. I lean into the wind, letting it clear out my head. Hoping it might erase a set of blue, blue, blue eyes from the deepest vaults of my memory.

After a few minutes, a thought occurs to me. I turn to ask, "How did you get a key?"

And how do I get one for myself?

"It's not mine, it's Henry's. We come up here all the time... I mean, *came* up here all the time. It was—" he breaks off mid-sentence, all light extinguished from his expression in the space of a few seconds .

"I'm sorry," I murmur. "I know the two of you are close."

His hazel eyes flash with thoughts I can't decipher. "We are. It's been... quite difficult."

"It's not the same, but... I lost my mom very suddenly two years ago. I didn't get to say goodbye because, even that last day, I didn't think it was real. It *couldn't* be real. She simply *couldn't* be dying." I suck in a sharp breath. "I guess what I'm trying to say is, I understand how hard it can be — what you're going through, right now. And I realize we don't know each other very well but, if you ever need someone to talk to..." I gesture around. "My turret is always open."

His smile returns. He takes a few steps toward me, hazel eyes never shifting away from mine. "Thank you, Emilia. I will definitely take you up on that offer. *Soon.*"

He reaches out his hand for mine. After a moment's hesitation, I place my palm against his. My heart flutters slightly as he laces our fingers together. And it feels... unquestionably nice.

Not like my heart might explode inside my chest from trying to contain all my emotions at once. Not like I'm at risk for having a stroke from the sheer strain of standing in his space. Not like my lungs aren't working properly because I keep forgetting to breathe around him.

Simple.

Easy.

Uncomplicated.

"Shall we descend?" he asks. Up close, his eyes have flecks of green and gold. They're stunning.

So why do I keep wishing they were blue?

I nod and smile brightly. "Sure. Let's go."

✦

ALDEN IS a picture-perfect gentleman as he walks me back to my room in the North Wing. We keep the conversation light, discussing the upcoming coronation. A flurry of activity unfolds around us as we pass through the Great Hall, where at least a dozen housekeepers are dusting chandeliers and polishing floors.

"There hasn't been a ball here for a long time," Alden murmurs, as we cross through an archway into the throne room. It reminds me of a church, full of stained glass and somber air. "Not since King Leopold and Queen Abigail threw a party to celebrate Henry's birth."

"You must've been very young."

"Little more than a baby." His grin is quick. "I don't remember much. Ava wasn't even born yet. Neither were you, come to think of it."

"Is that typical? To have so few balls?"

"King Leopold wasn't a fan of excess or debauchery." His eyes grow sad again. "Not like his son. Henry loved a good party. If he'd been crowned... his coronation would've been a celebration the likes of which Germania has never seen."

I'm quiet as we ascend the grand staircase up to the second floor, at a loss for what to say. Whenever he speaks of Henry, I feel like a total imposter — an unwanted changeling, swapped out for the rightful heir.

Alden seems to realize we've waded into uncomfortable

waters, because he suddenly squeezes my hand and brightens his tone. "See those suits of armor?"

I glance at the row of medieval-looking hollow knights, lining the hallway.

"Funny story…" He chuckles. "Once, maybe five years back, after a few too many rounds of Germanian ginger mules, we were all stumbling around the castle…"

By the time we round the corner toward my suite, he's got me laughing uproariously as he tells me about the time he, Chloe, Carter, and Henry got drunk, put on antique suits of armor, and ran through the halls at midnight, their battle cries waking up everyone in the entire castle.

"Then, Chloe fell over and couldn't get back up. The armor was so heavy, it took all three of us to stand her upright again."

I throw back my head and laugh. "Oh my god, please tell me there is photographic evidence."

Alden shakes his head, grinning. "Afraid not. Can you imagine if that ever leaked to the press? We would've been lambasted."

"I'd imagine Simms did some lambasting of his own, when he found out."

He laughs. "How right you are."

We've reached my door, but I hesitate in the hallway. "Alden… thank you."

"For what?" he asks, squeezing my hand.

"Taking my mind off things for a while." I shrug. "I haven't laughed this much in a long time."

"That's a crime." He steps closer, perfect teeth flashing. There's not a single hair out of place on his perfectly parted platinum head. "You have a wonderful laugh, Emilia."

He's not quite six feet tall, so when he leans his face down toward mine, the distance isn't all that far. I feel my mouth go dry, watching him come closer.

Is he going to kiss me?

Am I going to let him?

My questions never get answers — there's a bang from our left, loud enough to make me jump out of my skin. Alden and I both spin our heads to look and find the source of the sound standing in the doorway of his suite, hand still on the knob, glaring darkly in our direction.

Carter.

Just the sight of him is enough to make my heart pound a mad tattoo — even with him glaring at me like he wants to ring my neck. I'm not sure what expression is on my face, but whatever he sees when he takes in the sight of me and Alden makes his lip curl with disdain.

"Carter," Alden says in a light tone, but I notice how tense his shoulders are. "Good to see you, mate."

Carter's eyes cut to Alden, then drop down to where our hands are still interlaced. A muscle jumps in his cheek.

"Alden. What are you doing here... *mate?*"

The words are friendly — the voice he says them in are considerably less so. I pull my hand out of Alden's grip with a tug that makes his brows lift.

"Just getting to know our princess a bit better." Alden crosses his arms over his chest. "Seems she's been sorely neglected, these past few weeks."

I think Carter's head might actually explode, when he hears that. His eyes narrow to cerulean pinpricks. He's careful not to look at me.

"Is that so?"

I swallow nervously as Alden shifts his body weight forward. "She's your new sister — you should really take better care of her."

"Looks like you're handling things just fine, from where I'm standing."

I wish the floor would swallow me up.

I wish a meteor would strike the castle.

I wish Chloe would come around the corner.

Literally anything *to get me out of this conversation.*

"It's been a while since I've seen you," Alden says conversationally.

Carter doesn't respond except to shrug.

Alden's brows quirk. "What have you been up to?"

"Oh, just busy making up for lost time." His tone is lethally soft — thunder rumbling, the first hint of an impending storm. "After a week of isolation at the Lockwood Estate, where the hottest prospect was Patricia the fifty-year-old cook, I had a lot of..." He pauses. "...pent up *energy*..." A smirk. "I needed to blow off. Thankfully, the three Swedish models I met last night were more than happy to oblige."

I flinch.

Alden laughs, as if he understands only too well. "Ah. I'm sure the women of Vasgaard are relieved to have you fully operational again."

"Mmm." Carter's eyes flicker to mine and hold. "Maybe I'll bring the models to the coronation. See if I can make Octavia's head explode."

"You have a death wish, mate."

"Maybe I do." He's still looking at me, that intense gaze holding me captive more effectively than chains. I'm locked onto him in turn — pulse pounding, barely breathing. Wishing like mad that the feeling spreading through my veins resembled anything close to the indifference projected on my face.

Would it bother you, little sister? his eyes seem to ask. *Seeing me with someone else?*

Before I can do something stupid, like break down in tears, I rip my gaze away and turn to face Alden. My voice is so falsely bright, I barely recognize it as my own.

"This was so much fun, but I really should be getting back to work — that essay on social cognition isn't going to write itself. Thanks again for the distraction, Alden. I'll see you in a few days, at the coronation."

"Oh—" His brows lift, startled by my brusque departure. "Save me a dance, princess?"

"Of course. Though I can't promise I won't step on your toes."

Before he can say more, I pop up onto my tiptoes, deposit a quick kiss on his cheek, and turn to slip inside my room without once looking back at the man standing down the hall, watching me with laser-like focus. It's probably rude to close my door in Alden's face after he's been so kind to me, but I don't really have a choice — not unless I want a witness to the emotional break-down I'm about to have.

Shaking with rage and humiliation and, *yes*, a heady dose of unquenched yearning, I sink down to the floor, hands pressed over my face to contain my tears. They leak out through my fingers anyway, hot and furious as they streak down my cheeks.

This is insane, I scold myself, even as a sob rattles my chest. *You just had a perfect first date with a perfect man... and here you are, emotionally crippled by a two second interaction with your asshole stepbrother?*

Forget about Carter Thorne.

You only want him because you know you can't have him.

But even my lies aren't enough to comfort me. Because, deep down, I know I wanted him long before I became aware we'd be sharing a household and a father figure and a bedroom wall. Just as I know I'll *keep* wanting him, despite all the very valid reasons I shouldn't, until time eventually steals away my memories.

IT'S LATE.

Beneath the covers in my darkened bedroom, I do my best to drift off to sleep but my mind refuses to power down, no matter how long I press my cry-swollen eyes closed. It doesn't help that I can hear Carter moving on the other side of the wall: the low refrains of his music, his footsteps on the hardwood, the rush of water as he takes a shower. I try not to picture him under the torrent, his chiseled body glistening, steam fogging up the glass…

I fail.

Miserably.

Rolling over for the twentieth time, I punch my pillow into a more comfortable shape. Its ironic — I hated it when he was gone, but I think I like it even less now that he's back, one inconsequential wall dividing my bed from his.

I wonder if he can hear me, too.

If he heard my tears.

If he felt my grief.

If I'm driving him as crazy as he is me.

The wall goes silent, and I know he's finally turned in for the night. It's impossible not to think of him lying there in the dark, staring up at the ceiling, mere feet from me.

Is he thinking of me lying here, my legs tangled in the sheets, my thoughts tangled up in him? Or does he fantasize instead about his exploits with the three Swedish models he was so quick to throw in my face?

The low chime of my overhead speakers connecting to a new bluetooth device makes me sit straight up in bed, eyebrows arched to my hairline. A second later, my confusion compounds when music starts to drift into the dark room — a haunting, melancholic melody.

What the hell?

The song itself isn't strange; I instantly recognize its familiar strains from an old playlist. What's odd is the fact that *I'm* not the one playing it.

Utterly perplexed, I grab my tablet off the nightstand. The

screen is dark, no songs queued. Same with my cellphone. It's not until the lyrics start and my mind registers the song title — *Don't You Cry For Me* by Cobi — that the pieces finally click into place. I know exactly what's happening.

It's Carter.

He's doing this.

He's playing me a song.

Somehow, he's synced his phone to my speakers. I'm not entirely sure how, but as the words wash over me — *oh, don't you cry for me* — I'm far more concerned with another question.

Why?

Why would he do this?

To comfort me? To torture me?

To let me know he heard my tears through the wall and felt...

Shame? Pity? Fear? Hope? Need? Sorrow?

I sit there in the pitch black, my body paralyzed as my mind tumbles in circles, and allow every lyric to embed itself in my heart like a piece of shrapnel.

I'm torn from the truth that holds my soul...

Vaguely, I realize there are tears tracking down my cheeks. I can't summon the will to even wipe them away. Every ounce of my attention is fixed firmly on the music... and the man playing it for me.

For four full minutes, I listen.

I weep.

I wait.

Searching for answers; coming up empty.

The song fades out.

The bluetooth chimes again as he disconnects.

And then there is only silence in the room. But my mind — oh, my mind is roaring so loud with questions, I know there's not a chance in hell I'll be sleeping tonight.

What game are you playing, Carter?

CHAPTER SEVENTEEN

I'M GOING to throw up.

Coronation day has officially arrived and, with it, nausea like nothing I've ever felt before. I stand in my bedroom, strapped into a corset. It's cinched so tight I can hardly breathe, let alone eat.

Probably for the best. I'd hate to vomit in front of dignitaries from twelve neighboring countries, plus everyone with a title in all of Germanian society.

The buzzing of my phone is a welcome distraction. I walk over to the nightstand and feel my face go pale when the screen flashes the word HOME. Someone is calling from my landline, at the house in Hawthorne. The house no one except me has a key for.

My fingers shake as I press a button to accept the call.

"Hello?"

"Ems — please don't hang up."

I sigh. "Owen, I asked for space…"

"*Please!*" He sounds desperate. "If you never speak to me again after this, that's fine. But I need you to hear me out right now. Can you do that?"

"Did you break into my house to call me?"

There's a pause.

"Oh my god, you did! What the fuck, Owen?"

"You wouldn't take my calls," he snaps. "I had no choice."

"The choice was to *give me space*, like I asked for. You know, after you told the entire world about my identity and ruined my life. Remember that?"

"Ems..." The sadness in his voice claws at the steel wall I erected around my heart, the day he betrayed me. "I know it's not an excuse, but that day... Look, I'm not proud of it. I'd been drinking. I was upset. God, you're the most important person in my life and I could feel you slipping away, and... it fucking terrified me. I lost it."

"That doesn't justify what you did." My voice gets small. "You say I'm the most important person in your life, that I'm your best friend... but those are just words. If you don't have the actions to back them up..."

"I'm sorry, Emilia. I'm so fucking sorry. You don't understand—"

"I do understand! I do." My throat feels clogged. "But you're supposed to be the one who protects me. Instead, you hurt me worse than anyone."

"If you'll just hear me out, I swear I'll make it right—"

"I'm hanging up, now, Owen."

"NO!" His roar is so loud, I flinch back from the phone. "I need you to listen. I don't have a lot of time. Look, things may already be in motion and I'm not sure if I can stop them."

"What are you talking about?"

He curses lowly. "After you left, these past few weeks... I've started taking a more active role in the anti-monarchy groups on campus."

My heart pangs painfully. "Why are you telling me this? To hurt me even more? To dig the knife in deeper? It wasn't enough to tell the world who I am — now you're going to tell them how much you hate me?"

"No! You've got it all wrong, Ems. I only joined the group because I thought they might have answers about..." His voice drops low, as if he's scared to say the next words too loudly. "About the fire."

The whole world stops turning.

"*What*? You mean the fire here at the palace?"

"Yes," he murmurs. "Emilia... Not everyone in these anti-royalist groups is content to keep marching peacefully, holding signs and staging walk-outs. Some of them want to take things further."

"What do you mean?"

"Last year, at one of the meetings, I heard some of the guys saying that the simplest way to solve our problem was to eliminate the source: no more Lancasters, no more line of succession... no more monarchy."

"Are you saying what I think you're saying?" My voice is a whisper. "Owen..."

"I'm saying that I re-joined the group after you were pulled into this life, because if there's even a chance those guys weren't joking..." He blows out a breath. "I couldn't let you walk around with a target on your back. Not if I knew there was something I could do to protect you."

My chest aches. I don't know what to say. I hardly know which way is up, right now. Everything feels skewed, like the world has tilted on its axis.

"Ems? Are you still there?"

"I'm here." I force myself to take a deep breath — not an easy feat, in this corset. "Do you think... do you think there's really a chance they could be responsible for the fire?"

"I haven't found out anything definitive, yet. They trust me to some degree — especially after they saw me on the news, getting detained by the King's Guard outside Windsor Abbey for outing you to the press. I'm not privy to everything, though. I need more time, plain and simple. But with the coronation tonight..."

"You think something is going to happen."

"Everyone in Germania with even a drop of Lancaster blood will be in that castle. Plus, elite members from countless other monarchies. It would be a perfect target."

Horror fills me. He's right.

"I don't know what you expect me to do with this information. Linus will never cancel — not without a credible threat. And there's no way I'll be able to skip it."

"I know." He pauses. "Just... please be careful. If anything ever happened to you, I'd never forgive myself."

A tear slips from the corner of my eye and falls to the hardwood with a small splat. "I will."

"Good," he says, voice gruff. I know he's holding his emotions tightly in check. "Could you... do you think you could call me afterward? So I can hear your voice and know you're okay?"

"Sure," I whisper. "And Owen?"

"Yeah?"

"Thank you. For having my back, even when things are so messed up between us."

"Don't thank me, Ems. Just stay safe."

As PREDICTED, my warnings about security fall on deaf ears.

Linus is, evidently, far too busy to speak to me, so it's Simms who receives my frantic stream of worries. He stands in the small sitting room of my suite, arms crossed over a too-tight tuxedo, double chin jiggling pompously.

"Your Highness, I assure you, you will be perfectly safe. The King's Guard is fully prepared for all contingencies. The castle is secure." His eyes scan me up and down, clearly disapproving of my bathrobe and bare feet. "Now, I must attend to our royal guests and you must get ready — unless you are planning to wear *that* to the ceremony."

I roll my eyes. "No, Simms."

"Very good, princess. Then I will send in your hair and makeup team to assist you with final preparations. Please do not dally — guests are beginning to arrive and you're expected down in the throne room within the hour."

He leaves in a huff, a cloud of self-inflated ego lingering in his wake like bad cologne.

FORTY MINUTES LATER, I study myself in the mirror, hardly recognizing the girl staring back at me. The ballgown is truly a work of art — champagne satin and tulle with intricately embroidered lace appliqué that covers both sleeves and extends downward in shimmering whirls of gold. The bodice is tight fitted, showing off my curves like never before with the help of the stiff corset boning. The back dips low to reveal most of my spine before flowing out into a full skirt, complete with a two foot train.

In this dress, I actually look like a princess.

In this dress... I almost *feel* like a princess.

I'm thoroughly convinced the hair and makeup ladies have

magical powers, because no fairy godmother could've done any better — even with a wand. My eyes are lined with black and gold, making the green of my irises pop. My lips are stained a deep berry tone that's somehow glossy without being sticky. And my wild curls have been tamed into sleek mahogany coils — an up-do specifically designed to suit a crown.

Just the thought of what's to come makes my mouth press into a solemn line and my hands shake with nerves.

"The look lovely, Your Highness," the hairstylist says, smiling proudly. "Are you ready to go?"

No.

"Yes," I murmur, turning my back on the stranger in the mirror. "Let's go."

My heart is thudding out of my chest as I float down the hall toward the throne room, four members of the King's Guard in full uniform accompanying my every step. I can hear the swell of voices as I approach the grand staircase. The hall below comes into view and I fight to keep fear from showing on my face.

At the bottom of the polished stone stairs, at least four hundred subjects are seated, awaiting their new king in fine gowns and tuxedoes. I spot Carter and Chloe sitting in the aisle closest to the raised throne platform. A few rows back, the Sterling family is gathered, all four platinum blond heads easy enough to spot in the sea of people.

Their presence should be reassuring. Instead, it increases my anxiety tenfold.

When Lady Morrell and I walked through the ceremony yesterday in the empty throne room, I felt confident enough. That confidence has fled, now that I'm standing here in a ballgown, about to be a spectacle for the whole world to judge. The aisle seems so much longer from here, an endless strip of navy and gold carpet cutting straight through the middle of the crowd. I shiver at the idea of traversing it, all those eyes fixed upon me as I glide toward the throne.

Twenty-five steps down.

One hundred yards dead ahead.

Take your place on the stage.

Stop.

Smile.

Breathe.

Simms is staring pointedly at me from the other side of the landing, fully prepared to make my introduction to the crowd… but my feet are frozen. I can't move. I stand in the shadows, just out of sight, trying and failing to make myself take my first steps down those stairs. Visions of me tripping on the train of my dress and cartwheeling head over heels down twenty-five stone steps in front of the entire court play on a continuous loop inside my head.

"Are you nervous?"

The whispered words make my head whip around. I startle when I see Linus standing several feet from me, dressed in the ornate gold cloak of a king. His expression is grave, his eyes intent as they move over my face.

I jerk my chin higher and shake my head. I won't give him the satisfaction of knowing just how scared I am. After what he did, I'll never let my guard down around him again.

"You look lovely, Emilia." His green eyes, so like mine, seem to gleam in the dark. "Every inch the princess I always knew you were."

"A fancy dress doesn't make me a princess," I snap back. "By your standards, any noblewoman down in that room could hire a seamstress and call herself a queen."

"You're wrong, my dear. Nobility is not equivalent to royalty. One is a social class; the other a destiny. Nobles can be elevated in rank through money or marriage, opportunity or favor... but no one on earth can alter the blood running through your veins, Emilia Lancaster." Linus sounds more serious than I've ever heard him. "You bow to no one, Your Royal Highness."

We look at each other — father to daughter, king to heir — and before I can stop myself, I ask a question I've been mulling over since the minute I learned he existed.

"Why did you leave her?" My hands curl into tight fists. "Why did you leave *us*?"

He flinches almost imperceptibly, but doesn't balk. "Because... she asked me to."

"What?"

"Your mother asked me to leave."

No. He's lying.

"That's not what she told me."

"No, I wouldn't imagine so. I'm sure she told you I was a scoundrel and a rake, a middle-aged man with a wandering eye who seduced a woman too young for him by about twenty-five years." He sighs. "And that is all true. However, it is not the full story. And it's not the reason I did not raise you as my daughter."

"Then why?"

"Your mother wanted nothing to do with this life. Not me or my familial obligations, not the pretension or the pomp, not the strict rules and restrictions that come along with the crown. None of it." He pauses. "She was a free spirit. An artist. She would've been utterly miserable, confined within the role of Duchess of Hightower. I'm sure you can see that."

"But, you could've left her and still..."

"Still claimed you," he finishes for me. "You're correct. I could have. But your mother asked for complete separation. A *clean cut*, she called it. A chance for you to have a totally normal life, without any of this to bog you down."

"And you agreed? Just like that?"

"Regardless of what you might think of me… I loved your mother very much. I would've done anything she asked of me. Even cut myself out of her life. Even walk away from my chance to raise my own child."

"And I suppose you never regretted that choice, seeing as you married Octavia a few short years later and got two brand new step-kids to fill that father-shaped void in your life."

He sighs deeply, regret twisting his features. "I wish, daily, that I had chosen to do things differently. These past few weeks… to see the fine woman you have grown into, to witness the way you have handled an unprecedented situation with grace and poise, when a lesser person might've crumbled beneath the pressure… it has been a source of both great pride and deep remorse."

I pull in a stunned breath. Much as I'd love to pretend his words have no effect on me, I can't. My father is standing there saying things I've waited my whole life to hear. And maybe it makes me weak for even listening, maybe it makes me a fool for believing a word he says, after the things he's done in the past…

But it's no use.

You're such an idiot, I scold myself, even as my heart clenches and my eyes begin to sting. *Not everyone deserves a second chance.*

"Emilia." Linus takes a step forward, so we're chest to chest, and reaches down to gather my limp hands within his own. It's the closest we've ever come to an embrace. "I know you never would've chosen this path for yourself. But I truly believe that is why you are meant to take it." He pauses. "A very wise woman once told me, '*Those who actively seek out power are those who least deserve it.*'"

"Mom," I whisper, voice breaking. "Mom said that."

He nods. "I've never forgotten."

"*Give a crown to a king, he will treat the world as commoners. Give a crown to a common man, he will treat the world like kings,*" I recite from memory, smiling even though I want to cry.

"I vow to you, Emilia..." Linus breaks off, a painful cough rattling through his chest, but manages to gather himself again. "I will try to be the kind of king she would be proud of. However short my reign."

A tear rolls down my cheek. I hear Mom's voice in my head, mingling with his.

I love you, pure heart.

Stay bold.

My chin lifts. Eyes glossy, I hold his stare for a long moment. There's so much to say to him and yet, not a single word materializes on my tongue.

What do you say to the man whose absence has defined your whole life, when he's finally standing before you, seeking forgiveness?

He smiles softly at me, his own eyes perilously wet, and I know he understands the meaning buried beneath my silence. In truth, I'm still not ready to forgive him for the choices he's made... even if I'm beginning to understand his justifications in making them.

Our road so far has been rocky. Fraught with thorny bushes and false turns. But perhaps someday... there's a chance we can move forward. On a new path, forged by circumstance, with cautious respect from both sides.

Not today.

But *someday*.

"Linus!" a cold, female voice snaps from the shadows, shattering the moment. "What on earth are you doing over here? I've been waiting with Gerald for five minutes."

We both turn to watch as Octavia strides toward us, her fitted

185

blue dress stunning against the fiery shade of her hair. Her eyes slide to mine.

"You are supposed to be on the stairs already, girl."

A week ago, I might've dropped my eyes to the floor. Avoided her stare, shied away from confrontation. But no more. Lifting my chin, I stare cooly into her eyes.

"My name is not *you* or *girl*. It is Emilia Victoria Lancaster. I suggest you start using it."

Ignoring the stunned look on her face, I set my shoulders proudly and brush past her with every ounce of grace and poise I can muster.

Lady Morrell would be so proud.

My heart thunders as I come to a stop at the edge of the landing. The stairs spill in front of me, a waterfall of stone. I pull in a shallow breath that strains the confines of my corset before giving Simms a small nod.

I'm ready.

He announces my arrival in a booming voice that barely registers in my ringing ears. A hush falls over the crowd below. Every head in the audience turns to look at me. There's a collective gasp as they take in the sight of my resplendent gold gown drifting down the stairs, one careful step at a time.

I keep my eyes dead ahead and attempt to maintain a stately pace. A hint of relief stirs inside me when I make it to the bottom without tripping on the massive train or stumbling on my high heels... at least, until I look forward at the gauntlet remaining before me.

My mother's voice is with me like a drumbeat as I take those first steps down the aisle. I set my pace by each syllable as I walk, feeling eyes on me from all sides.

Stay bold.

Stay bold

Stay bold

Eighty yards.

Fifty yards.

Twenty yards.

The throne creeps ever closer, the crowd around me a mass of faceless strangers. I'm nearing the end of this long, dreadful parade when I sense a set of eyes on me from the front row, strong enough to draw my focus. I tell myself not to look at him, not to yield to the tractor-beam of his stare… but as I pass within a few feet of his chair, my own eyes shift without executive permission. They lock on his, bright blue and burning with unmasked longing and for the first time since Simms said my name…

My feet falter.

It's just a slight bobble before I recover; a stumble so small, I doubt anyone even notices. Except Carter. He's watching me so intently, I know there's not a detail of my dress he hasn't memorized, not a single move I make that escapes his hyper-alert focus.

Swallowing hard, I tear my gaze from his and start up the three wide steps onto the pavilion, where the archbishop is waiting in full regalia. I nod respectfully to him as I take my spot in front of the small, ornate chair to the right of the gilded throne. I don't risk looking at the front row again, instead sweeping my eyes across the expanse, taking it all in.

My kingdom.

Every face in the crowd is turned to mine. They appear awed as they behold me. As though they're witnessing something truly spectacular. It's easily the most surreal moment of my entire life. My heartbeat pounds between my ears louder than a battle drum the longer I stand there — all eyes fixed on me, taking my measure in turn.

Their princess.

Thankfully, Simms voice draws their attention away before the pressure can crack my composure — booming out to announce Octavia's entrance. Everyone shifts in their seats to watch her, the picture of regal poise as she begins her procession down the stairs. She soaks in every ounce of attention, her steps tiny, her pace glacial. I think I lose three or four years of my life, just waiting for her to take her place beside me on the stage.

Really putting the queen *in drama queen, if you ask me.*

Simms voice booms out one final time.

"His Royal Majesty Linus Lancaster, King of Germania…"

Every member of the audience climbs to their feet to greet him, a sign of respect reserved only for the highest echelon of the monarchy. Linus looks every bit a king as he makes his dignified procession down the aisle toward us. His eyes meet mine for the briefest of moments as he steps up onto the throne pavilion. I see a flash of warmth and pride before he looks away to greet the archbishop. Bowing his head, he takes a shuddering breath as he kneels upon the plush cushion at the center of the stage.

And so it begins.

THE ESSENTIAL ELEMENTS of a Germanian coronation have remained largely unchanged for the past thousand years: an hour-long ceremony of acclaim, anointment, and sworn oaths to uphold the law, the church, and above all, the loyal subjects of the land.

Linus' voice is strong and clear as he accepts his responsibility. When he rises, an elaborate crown sitting upon his head, the applause is so loud, I hear the crystal chandeliers rattling perilously overhead. Lady Morrell instructed me most firmly that I was not to clap — *a princess does not cheer with the masses; do endeavor to maintain a somber countenance* — but I can't help myself from smiling.

In a sort of daze, I watch as the archbishop moves on to inaugurate Octavia as Queen Consort — a simpler, shorter version of the same process. (I assure you, my somber countenance is *firmly* in place when the room applauds for her.)

Then, terrifyingly… it's my turn.

Kneeling with my hands clasped tightly, I stare into the dull brown eyes of the bishop as I repeat back the words of fealty I've spent the past few days practicing in my bathroom mirror.

To my great surprise, as I speak my oath, the blind sense of panic fades. My pulse slows to a steady tempo. My voice doesn't shake, the words crystal clear as they rings out in the silent room.

"I, Emilia Victoria Lancaster, do pledge my sovereign allegiance to the people of Germania as heir apparent to the throne. In this role, I vow to uphold law and justice with mercy, to maintain the doctrine, worship, and discipline of both church and state, and to preserve all such rights and privileges of each man, woman, and child under my dominion." I take a deep breath and bow my head. "All that which I have promised, I will perform and keep to the fullest extent of my power. So help me God."

The room is so silent, you could hear a button drop.

The archbishop anoints my forehead with holy oil, his thumb slippery against my skin. I inhale involuntarily when he lifts the sparkling tiara from an ornate box to his left. It's heavy with gold and diamond; heavier still with importance as he sets it down upon my head. It settles against my hair, glittering in the light, a perfect complement to my gown.

As I rise and turn to greet my countrymen, I'm met with a forceful wave of applause. They cheer and clap, eyes feverish with unconditional excitement as they behold me.

Their heir apparent.

Their future queen.

I have done nothing to earn their love. Yet here I stand, a product of divine right, acclaimed and adored for no reason at all. A fraud, collecting credit for absolutely nothing except the surname on my birth certificate.

The smile wavers on my lips. The pulse jumps in my veins. And the beautiful crown upon my head begins to feel like something else entirely.

A golden lie.

A dirty halo.

CHAPTER EIGHTEEN

"Hot damn, E! You look fucking incredible! That dress is a wet dream."

"Um." I blink at Chloe. "Thank you... I think?"

"Trust me, it's a compliment."

"She's right," Alden cuts in smoothly, stepping up to me with a smile. His eyes are shining. "You look absolutely perfect, princess."

My smile wavers. "Please, don't call me that."

His brows lift in confusion.

I glance away, back to Chloe, and find her squinting at the diamonds on my tiara. Her cherry red lips — the same shade as the mermaid-style dress she's wearing — are parted in pure lust.

"You're going to let me try it on later, right?"

I snort. "I don't think I'm allowed to, actually. Pretty sure it goes back into the royal vault as soon as the party ends."

"Then I suppose we'd better make the most of the moment." Alden's hand extends. "If it's not too forward of me... may I have the first dance?"

"Oh," I murmur, blushing deeply. "Of course."

He beams as he tucks my hand in the crook of his arm and leads me out onto the dance floor. I glance around at the Great Hall, telling myself I'm taking in the sights — not scanning restlessly for a dark head of hair and broad, tuxedoed shoulders amongst the throng of guests.

There's no sign of him anywhere. And I can't help noticing that Ava is suspiciously absent, as well.

It doesn't matter.

It doesn't matter.

It doesn't matter.

Pushing thoughts of Carter Thorne from my head, I force myself to appreciate the beauty of the ballroom. The space has been impressively transformed, full to the brim with fresh flower arrangements and white linen table cloths and shining silver candlesticks. Sharply uniformed waitstaff distribute champagne flutes to everyone in the crowd. An eight-piece string band offers musical accompaniment to the many couples already whirling around elegantly at the center of the room.

Alden and I take our place amongst them. I hardly breathe as he leads me through my first ever waltz — well, with anyone besides Lady Morrell, which I'm relatively certain doesn't count. He's a much more exciting partner, leading my turns with ease, steering my every move as though there are marionette strings attached to my toes. I find after a while, I'm actually enjoying myself as we glide to the tempo.

"I can't believe you lied to me," he whispers in my ear as the waltz comes to an end.

"What?"

His smile is ultra white. "You're a lovely dancer. You've not tread on my feet even once."

"Give it time."

"Does that mean I can persuade you to dance with me again?"

I open my mouth to agree, but the words are cut off by a lightly accented voice from the left.

"Unfortunately, the princess cannot dance with you," a young man I don't recognize says, bowing slightly as he beholds me, his brown eyes sparkling. "As she will be dancing with me."

"Oh?" I arch a brow. "And you are…?"

"Westley Egerton, Baron of Frenberg. It's an honor to make your acquaintance, Your Royal Highness."

"Just Emilia, please."

His brows shoot up in shock at such familiarity. Lady Morrell would be positively scandalized by my impropriety, but I don't care. I'm so tired of being called *Your Highness* I could spit. And the night has only just begun.

"Princess Emilia it is, then," Egerton says tactfully, smiling as he extends a hand. "Shall we?"

With an apologetic glance at Alden, I take his outstretched hand and allow myself to be pulled into another spirited dance. Feeling the weight of many male stares, I have a creeping suspicion his won't be my only offer the evening…

♛

My hunch, as it turns out, is correct.

Two hours later, my feet are aching as yet another suitor from some place I can't remember the name of steers me around the dance floor. Unfortunately for me, unlike Alden, this particular earl does not possess even an ounce of lightness of foot — as evidenced by the fact that he's already trampled on mine at least three times.

"Apologies again, Your Highness."

I hide my wince with a fake smile. "Not a problem."

Chloe grimaces at me over the shoulder of the handsome lord she's dancing with. I try to smile back, but it turns to another scowl of pain as his considerable weight comes down on my toes.

"Deepest apologies, yet again—"

I set my teeth in a grimace and pray it's almost over. I'm exhausted from smiling benignly and making small talk with strangers; from being mauled by middle-aged lords with sagging bellies and sour breath; from fending off scathing comments from their wives during the brief interludes I've managed to escape the dance floor for a fortifying sip of champagne.

"Please forgive me, Princess," the earl is saying, but my attention is suddenly elsewhere — snagging on something in the crowd that makes my heart race at twice its normal rate. Something I haven't locked eyes on all night, despite my constant search.

There's a man standing at the edge of the dance floor. He's got a glass of bourbon in his grip, but his eyes are on me. Even from this distance, I know he can see the way I wince when the Earl of Toe-Crushing lives up to his nickname once more.

"So sorry, so sorry…"

I open my mouth on auto-pilot, prepared to accept his most recent apology, but the words evaporate from my tongue. I can't speak, can't even breathe. Every fiber in my being is fully occupied, watching as Carter slowly drains the bourbon from his glass and steps out onto the floor. There's a darkly determined look on his face as he crosses toward us, cutting a path through the sea of swirling couples without ever removing his eyes from mine. He moves like a predator, smooth muscles and lithe strength in an immaculately-tailored tuxedo.

Holy.

Shit.

My feet go still and the earl stumbles off balance, his hand falling away from my lower back. I don't even bother apologizing as Carter comes to a stop beside us. His dark brows are pulled inward.

"Can I cut in?"

He doesn't wait for permission. He simply steps into our space, slides his arms around my body, and tugs me out of the earl's fumbling hold. My lips part on a gasp as my body collides briefly with the hard planes of his chest. I press them firmly together as my right hand interlaces with his, my left sliding up to rest lightly on his shoulder.

"What do you think you're doing?" I hiss as we begin to move.

"Just being a good brother." He pauses meaningfully, eyes glittering with leashed violence — at me, at our situation, at the whole damn world. "Saving my sister from permanent foot damage."

"Carter..."

"You'd rather I left you to that great oaf?" he mutters, eyes narrowing. "Fine. I'm sure I can call him back—"

"Don't you dare," I snap.

He smirks.

I blow out an exasperated sigh and give myself over to the dance. And it's strange — we're surrounded by hundreds of people but, somehow, in the circle of his arms, I'm able to convince myself it's just the two of us. A dance all our own, without regret or repercussion.

We move together flawlessly — miles more in sync than even my most accomplished suitors. It's as though my body recognizes his, as though he knows every step I'm going to make before it happens. As the waltz progresses, our spins and turns bringing our bodies closer and closer, the sliver of air between our faces begins to simmer with so much tension, it's hard to breathe properly. His hand tightens on my waist, flexing against the gold fabric of my dress, and I know he feels it, too.

I just hope no one watching from the crowd can see the way my pulse is pounding, can sense the slight hitch in my breath whenever I pull a shallow gulp of air into my lungs.

Just two siblings, sharing a celebratory dance.

Totally innocent.

His face is set in a polite mask, but his eyes — they singe me like a fiery brand. He hasn't looked at me like this since the night we crossed an unspeakable boundary, back at the Lockwood Estate. I worry as soon as this dance ends, he'll never look at me like that again. That, as soon as the notes fade into silence, he'll throw that wall back into place — the one made of callous indifference, that's so terribly effective at shutting me out.

Time is running short. Each slide of the violin bow against its strings carries us one note closer to the end of this moment. The end of *us*. So, before I can stop myself, before I can remember the reason why those careful walls exist between us in the first place... I ask a reckless question. A question that's been killing me each night as I lie in bed, waiting for a bluetooth chime that never comes.

"The song." My throat convulses. "*Why?*"

The final notes play out, and our steps taper off into stillness. He still hasn't given me an answer. In my peripherals, I sense couples around us pulling apart, exiting the dance floor in the brief interlude between songs... but we don't move. Neither of us is ready to let go. Because we both know, the moment we do...

It's over.

"Why?" I beg, a break in my voice.

He stares at me with his jaw clenched tight for so long, I don't think he's going to answer. When he finally speaks, his tone is carefully stripped of all emotion.

"Because the only thing I hated more than seeing you with him... was making you cry over me."

His words hit me like a physical punch. My hands drop away

from him. My eyes are full of tears when I shake my head and whisper, "Then you'd better look away."

The last thing I see before I turn and race off the dance floor is Carter's face, crumbling with defeat and despair. My feet don't slow as I brush past several waiting suitors, eager to claim my next dance. The facade I've kept in place all evening is unraveling with an alacrity that scares me. If I'm going to hold myself together, I need air that doesn't smell like bourbon, spice, and smoke. I need space that's not thrumming with acute anguish. I need time enough to forget the feeling of forbidden hands on my skin.

So incredibly wrong.

So utterly right.

Leaving the ballroom behind with a series of muttered excuses, I don't stop until I've found my way outside into the castle gardens. It's dark and cold in the late October night — far too chilly for any other party guests to brave the elements. The three King's Guard keeping watch at the doors don't try to stop me as I run down the winding path, long train whipping out behind me like a flag. I revel in the silent solitude as I drag uneven breaths into my lungs.

I'm not even sure where I'm headed until I find myself stepping into the glass greenhouse at the center of the courtyard. It's warmer inside. There's no light except that of the full moon shining overhead. It takes a moment for my eyes to adjust, squinting until the shapes of various plants and flowers come into view. There's something almost haunted about this place, lit only by starlight. Closed off from the rest of the world.

Brushing the worst of the dirt off a slate workman's table, I prop myself against it and drop my head into my hands. The clatter of my crown falling to the flagstones makes me jump — I'd completely forgotten it was on my head.

Oops.

I crack open my eyes, already bending to retrieve it... and freeze as I find myself staring not at a dirty greenhouse floor, but into the turbulent blue eyes of the man who's just crouched down at my feet. I didn't even hear him follow me in, but there he is — Lord Carter Thorne. On his knees with my tiara clutched gently in his big hands, looking up at me like I'm the source of all his pain and all his passion.

Shadows play over his features as I reach out, trembling like a leaf, and wrap my fingers around the tiara. He doesn't relinquish his hold — even when I tug lightly. Instead, he rises, finding his feet in one smooth motion, stepping forward into my space... And then, the crown is clattering back to the stones at our feet, utterly forgotten, because without another thought or breath or beat of hesitation, Carter reaches out, hauls me into his chest, and crushes his mouth to mine.

Passion explodes violently, a tsunami that washes in without warning and submerges us completely. Our hands claw and tear, desperate to get closer after so much time suffering in separate agony. My fingers dig into his back, hard enough to bruise. His lips claim mine, savage enough to leave them swollen.

There is no room for reasonable questions or sound arguments. Not anymore. We have flown past the point of no return, to a place were the only thing that matters is this.

Us.

Now.

His kiss is a broken promise on borrowed time. His touch is faulty fuse struck with the hottest match. We possess all the potential in the world without an ounce of fulfillment. We are a lost cause, doomed before our inception. And still, I cannot stop myself from shoving the tuxedo jacket off his shoulders, to the dirty ground. Just as he can't prevent his hands from lifting me up onto the slate table.

My legs part beneath the thick layers of tulle as he bunches it by my waist, so he can step closer.

Closer.

Never close enough.

My need for him is so strong, I can hardly see straight as my shaking hands slide down his chest to trace the throbbing outline of his cock through the thin fabric. The ache between my thighs magnifies as I feel his shaft swell beneath my touch. *God...* he's so huge, so *hard*, it's difficult to believe I'm the one who's sparking this reaction within him.

He growls my name as his hands clutch me harder, lips dropping to suck the sensitive skin of my neck. The nip of teeth against my jugular vein, where my pulse races double speed, has my back arching like a bowstring.

Fingers grasping blindly, I fumble with the buttons of his pants, then struggle to slide his zipper down. I need to free him, to *feel* him heavy within the grip of my hands, no barriers left between us. I need to watch him come undone beneath my touch, just as he's undoing me. I need him inside me, under my skin, embedded so deep he'll never fully leave me.

His hands tangle in my hair as he kisses me again, ruining my perfect up-do in an instant. I don't give a shit. Our lips never part, even as I pull him into my hand and begin to pump his length, rhythmic strokes that draw deep groans of pleasure from the back of his throat.

With a sudden growl, he tears his lips from mine and shoves me back, flat against the table. Before I can blink, he's out of my reach, kneeling on the ground between my legs. His dark head disappears beneath my voluminous skirts, his hands roughly shove my knees apart. I cry out when his fingers delve into the flimsy fabric of my underwear and tear it clear off my body, the intricate stitches no match for his impatience.

I don't even have time to be shocked by his savage action. My focus narrows to the broad fingers stroking my inner thighs as he hitches my legs over his shoulders. When he leans in, his mouth sucking on my clit like he's been starving for me, I swear my whole damn world ceases to exist. There's nothing left but this — his lips feasting on me, my back arching up off the table. Pleasure spikes in a dizzying bolt, my thighs clenching around him as he fucks me slowly with his tongue.

The orgasm slams into me without warning, so fast I'm unprepared for it. I cry out as I come, loudly enough to draw unwanted attention. Carter swiftly rises to cover my mouth with his, swallowing my cries as his hands finish the job his lips began. His fingers slide into my soaked core, first one finger, then two, working with expert precision as waves of pleasure crash through me, over and over, a never-ending tide. I'm moaning, clutching wildly at him as I taste myself on his tongue, desperate for more even as my whole body trembles with aftershocks.

Our eyes meet in the darkness and I see my own lust reflected back at me — so strong, it's almost painful. I grab his shirt and pull him fully down on top of me, his heavy weight settling between my thighs. Tulle bunches around my waist in a thick layer, but I hardly notice as my legs wind around his back.

"Emilia," he groans, face suddenly tortured. "Are you sure?"

"I'm on the pill," I whisper, kissing him again. Sliding my hands into his hair. Reveling in the delicious weight of his hard, hot body, pressing me down against the cool slate.

"You know that's not what I mean. Once we do this…"

His expression is composed as he hesitates, but the rapid rise and fall of his chest gives him away, as does the tension in his shoulders when his hands plant themselves on either side of my face. I feel the hard head of his shaft brush the slickness between my thighs, and that merest hint of him is nearly enough to trigger another orgasm.

"Carter…" I reach down between us, encircle my hand

around his pulsing length, and maneuver him until he's poised perfectly at my entrance. *"I'm sure."*

Groaning with need, he slams himself home without another instant of doubt, entering me in a brutal thrust that jerks my whole body several inches up the table. I'm unable to tame the screams of pleasure that fly from my throat as he moves inside me, filling me so fully, I think my body might break in two. He fucks me like a man possessed, each stroke deeper than the last.

"Emilia."

He growls my name like a prayer. Like a promise. Like a vow.

His tongue spears into my mouth, moving to the same rhythm as his cock. His eyes are wilder than I've ever seen them — holding mine captive as we move together, thrust for thrust.

We are dancing on the edge of a blade that's liable to slice us both in two at any instant, but I don't care. Right now, there's just him and me and this table. No past, no future. No names, no labels. Just lust and need and maybe, if I look a little deeper, something more.

Something that scares me a million times more than anything else I've faced, tonight.

When I orgasm again, it's even more powerful than the first time. Carter follows me over the edge of pleasure mere seconds later, my name exultant on his lips as he spills himself inside me. And as we lie there in the aftermath, breathing hard with the glass of the greenhouse fogging around us and the moon a pale spotlight overhead, we hold each other so tight, it's almost easy to forget that in a few short minutes...

We're going to have to let go.

CHAPTER NINETEEN

WE DRESS IN THE DARKNESS, not speaking as we brush dirt from our expensive clothes, straighten our mussed hair, refasten our buttons. I can't quite meet his eyes as he bends to retrieve my tiara from the stone floor.

"Here."

I stare at the literal reminder of responsibility, a tangible reality check cradled within his hands, and feel my heart stutter inside my chest.

"Thank you," I whisper rather haltingly, reaching out to take it from him. Hoping it's not crooked, I set it back on top of my head. I press my eyes closed to keep my emotions in check as I force out the next words. "We should probably head back."

I swear he makes a low sound of rage, but when my eyes flash open, he looks totally composed. The picture of indifference.

"They'll come looking for me, if I'm gone too long."

He snorts, but otherwise doesn't respond.

My eyes narrow. "Do you have something to say?"

"No. You want to go back in there, that's fine. But if you think I'm about to follow you, to stand there on the sidelines, watching you flirt with every man in a six hundred mile radius—"

"Do you honestly think I like this?" I cut him off sharply, temper rising to match his. "Do you think I enjoy being passed from hand to hand like some prized breeding mare, when the only person I want to be with—" I bite my lip to contain the dangerous words, so hard I'm surprised it doesn't split down the center.

"What's your suggestion, Emilia?" Carter's eyes have gone so dark, I hardly recognize him. "Let me guess — forget this ever happened? Go back to being enemies?" He snorts. "'Cause that worked really fucking well for us the last time we tried, didn't it? Two weeks of space, then a quick screw on a workbench during your bloody coronation!"

My spine snaps straight. "*A quick screw.* Was that all this was to you?"

"You tell me, Emilia." He leans in, gaze trapping mine. "What was this? A beginning or an ending?"

"*I don't know*, all right? This wasn't supposed to happen. God..." I shake my head, feeling my emotions unravel. Confusion, despair, and longing are tearing at me with violent talons. I want nothing more than to take those three steps forward, to throw myself into the circle of his arms and bury my head against his chest. But losing myself in him won't solve a damn thing. In fact...

Losing myself in him is exactly why we're in this mess.

"Carter," I say in a broken voice. "Please..."

"Please what, princess?"

"You know that if things were different—"

"But they're not," he says flatly, expression shuttering into a callous mask I recognize all too well.

"No. They're not," I echo, wondering how things got so turned around so incredibly fast.

Five minutes ago, I was in his arms.

Now, we can barely look at each other.

"Go on then, Your Highness." He jerks his chin toward the doors. "Back to your precious party."

"Carter—"

"*Go.*"

I flinch at the coldness in his voice. Before the tears start flowing, I steel my shoulders, straighten my ballgown, and walk out the door, back into the bitter night.

THE PARTY FEELS garish and gaudy, too loud and too bright after the poignant passion of the dark greenhouse. I float through the crowd, face set in a frigid mask, nodding hello to people as I pass. Chloe tries to wave me over from a table in the corner, but I avoid her eyes. I know she'll see instantly that something is wrong, and press me for details. I'm so dazed, I don't notice Linus and Octavia until I've nearly bumped straight into them.

"Emilia," my father says, scanning my flushed face and messy hair. "Are you all right?"

I nod. "Of course. Why wouldn't I be?"

"We've been looking for you for the past twenty minutes," Octavia snaps. "We need you on the platform for the champagne toast."

"Sorry," I murmur halfheartedly. I can't seem to summon the energy to care about anything, at the moment. Especially not Octavia's petty problems.

She stomps toward the small dais. Linus and I trail in her wake.

"I'm sorry about my wife," he murmurs, too low for her to hear. "She wasn't always so uptight about punctuality."

"I think it has less to do with me being late than it does *me*, in general." I sigh. "Everything I do seems to displease her. I swear, I'm not even trying."

We lapse into a short silence. Just before we ascend onto the small stage, where a platter bearing three crystal champagne flutes waits, he meets my eyes.

"The sooner you let go of the idea that you can please everyone, the better off you will be, Emilia. This life we live... it's not about contentment. Progress rarely comes about with any sort of peace of mind. And, as you'll soon learn... real royalty isn't about achieving that much-lauded *happily ever after*. It's about duty and obligation to something larger than yourself. To crown and country."

I swallow hard, unable to retort.

"After you," he murmurs, gesturing me toward the stairs.

In silence, I take my place beside Octavia on the platform. Linus steps between us to address the crowd. My eyes scan the sea of faces, looking for Carter, but I don't see him anywhere.

"Thank you all for coming here tonight, to celebrate this occasion. It has been a dark time for Germania. We have suffered tremendous losses, the likes of which we will struggle for years to recover from. But we cannot abandon faith. We cannot lose ourselves in the darkness. Now, more than ever, we must band together. A united front. A unified kingdom." He reaches out and plucks two of the champagne glasses from the tray. Passing one to me and the other to Octavia, he takes the final flute for himself and lifts it into the air.

"*Non sibi sed patriae*," he calls, voice ringing out with hope and strength. "Not for self, but country. May we all strive to embody that core Germanian value each day, as we move forward into a bright future."

He takes a hearty gulp of his champagne. As is customary, the rest of the hall waits for him to finish his sip before joining.

"*Non sibi sed patriae,*" we all echo, as he lowers his glass. "Long live King Linus! Long live King Linus! Long live King Linus!"

The chant goes on for quite some time, until he waves to signal quiet. His flute raises again. "Thank you, my friends. Now, let us join in a drink, not as king and subject, but as friends."

More cheers break out as the crowd sips their champagne. I lift my own flute to my lips, but pause when I hear a strangled sound from Linus. Wide-eyed, I glance over and see his face turning a deep, mottled purple color. Foam is gathering at one corner of his mouth.

"Linus? Oh, god, *Linus!*"

The flute drops from his hand, glass shattering on impact. He claws at his throat, suddenly desperate for oxygen as his windpipe swells shut. It's as though he's choking on thin air. All I can do is watch as his body crumples to the dais like a rag doll.

"HELP!" I scream, falling to my knees beside him, my flute abandoned. I stare down in horror, wishing I knew what to do. "PLEASE HELP US!"

Octavia is wailing something from his other side, but I pay her no mind. I look into my father's face, grabbing his hand tight inside my own.

"Hang on," I whisper. "Just hang on. Do you hear me? Help is coming."

But even as I tell him to stay strong, the light is beginning to fade from his eyes. The white froth at his mouth is thicker now, tinged pink with flecks of blood as it dribbles down his chin to pool on the platform beneath us.

No.

No, no, no.

A tear falls from my eyes down onto his face.

"You cannot die," I forbid him, voice breaking. "The

kingdom needs you." I suck in a breath. "*I* need you. I'm not ready to do this without you. Do you hear me, Linus? Do you hear me, Dad?"

His chest rattles.

His lids close.

His jaw slackens.

And in the space of a breath…

In the length of a heartbeat…

In the blink of a deep green eye…

A crown changes hands once more.

THE END

…for now.

My dear reader,

Adele voice

Hellooooo from the other sideeee!

Thank you so much for reading. There are literally millions of other books out there you could've spent your last few hours immersed in, so I am deeply touched you chose to pick up mine. I sincerely hope you enjoyed the first installment of Emilia's story!

Don't miss **TORRID THRONE**, the sequel to **DIRTY HALO**, coming Fall 2018.

PS: If you enjoyed this book, please take a minute to leave a review on your favorite e-retailer. xx

Non sibi sed patriae,
Evie

PLAYLIST

1. **Castle** — Halsey
2. **Royals** — Lorde
3. **Young and Beautiful** — Lana Del Rey
4. **King and Lionheart** — Of Monsters and Men
5. **Kingdom Fall** — Claire Wyndham
6. **Light Me Up** — Ingrid Michaelson
7. **Listen** — Claire Guerreso
8. **Everybody Wants to Rule the World** — Lorde
9. **Arsonist's Lullaby** — Hozier
10. **Leave the Door Wide Open** — Black English
11. **Don't You Cry For Me** — Cobi
12. **Half Light** — BANNERS
13. **Beggin For Thread** — BANKS
14. **Halo** — Ane Brun (feat. Linnea Olsson)
15. **Call It What You Want** — Taylor Swift

ABOUT THE AUTHOR

EVIE EAST hates many things -- including cats, weak coffee, people who don't use their directionals while driving, and writing bios about herself in the third person. Her full name is Genevieve, but no one calls her that. (*Seriously. Don't call her that. She won't answer.*) Like any true bookworm, she enjoys fictional people more than real ones. Evie resides in New England and firmly believes it is the best place on earth.

She is currently at work on **TORRID THRONE**, a sequel to **DIRTY HALO**. Look for it Fall 2018.

Make sure to sign up for Evie's BOOK BLAST, a monthly newsletter featuring sneak peeks, exclusive giveaways, and more!

CLICK HERE TO SUBSCRIBE
&
MAKE SURE TO FOLLOW EVIE:

CPSIA information can be obtained
at www.ICGtesting.com
Printed in the USA
LVHW08s2107280818
588394LV00011B/1168/P